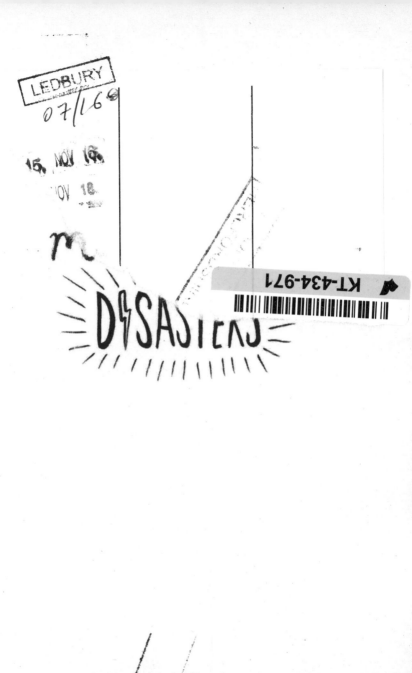

LOVE

& other man~made

DISASTERS

Nicola Doherty

Indigo

Orion Children's Books

First published in Great Britain in 2016 by Hodder and Stoughton
1 3 5 7 9 10 8 6 4 2

Text copyright © Nicola Doherty 2016

The moral rights of the author have been asserted.

All characters and events in this publication, other than those clearly in the public domain, are fictitious and any resemblance to real persons, living or dead, is purely coincidental.

All rights reserved.

No part of this publication may be reproduced, stored in retrieval system, or transmitted, in any form or by any means, without the prior permission in writing of the publisher, nor be otherwise circulated in any form of binding or cover other than that in which it is published and without a similar condition including this condition being imposed on the subsequent purchaser.

A CIP catalogue record for this book
is available from the British Library.

ISBN: 978 1 5101 0037 4

Typeset by Input Data Services Ltd, Bridgwater Somerset

Printed and bound in Great Britain by
CPI Group (UK) Ltd, Croydon, CR0 4YY

The paper and board used in this book are
made from wood from responsible sources.

Indigo
An imprint of
Hachette Children's Group
Part of Hodder and Stoughton
Carmelite House
50 Victoria Embankment
London EC4Y 0DZ

An Hachette UK Company

www.hachette.co.uk

To my mother, who always looks on the bright side

1

These are just some of the things I'm afraid of.

1. Climate change.
2. World War Three.
3. Terrorist attacks.
4. Getting cancer and dying.
5. Getting cancer and dying without ever falling in love. I'm pretty sure that if I get cancer, there won't be a gorgeous guy with one leg in my support group.
6. My hair getting caught in a bus or car door and strangling me.
7. Being kidnapped and murdered by a serial killer and buried in someone's back garden.
8. Failing all my A levels. Or doing badly and it all goes wrong from there and I can't get a job and have to live at home for ever – wherever home is.

9. Civilisation breaking down and me dying because I don't know the right berries to eat.
10. Zombies. Obviously they don't exist, but still.
11. Skiing and other dangerous sports.
12. Urban foxes. They know how to get inside houses, and there was one on the news that mugged a man for his quiche.
13. My parents getting divorced and Mum remarrying.
14. Mum marrying a man who makes us go skiing with his twins.

So far only 13 and 14 have actually happened.

2

I wish I was, literally, anywhere but here.

OK, I take that back. That's a misuse of the word 'literally'. I wouldn't want to be living in a post-apocalyptic wasteland. But at least there I'd be forced to grow up quickly and I'd be a free agent instead of being strapped into the back seat of a rented Mercedes on a motorway in Austria, between two eight-year-old boys.

'Everyone OK in the back?' Mum asks, turning her head round to beam at us. That's typical of my mum: she makes unpopular decisions and then wants reassurance that they're fine. Such as asking me to be a flower girl at her wedding to Ed. Whoever heard of a seventeen-year-old flower girl?

'Juno? All OK?'

I have to clear my throat because it's so long since I said anything. I'm about to say, 'I'm fine,' when Ed starts,

'Simon? Simon? OK yeah, I can hear you. So what did Boots say?'

Mum is still looking at me: in response I widen my eyes, point to Ed with my chin and flatten myself against the back seat, clinging to my seat belt. Mum widens her eyes back at me, and turns round again. I don't need to say anything; she knows how I feel about people who talk on the phone while driving. Even if it is hands-free.

I'm not paranoid: I'm safety-conscious. In a cinema, I always try to sit near the fire exits, and I also check for the best escape route in case there's a hostage-type situation. I wear natural fibres on a plane, as synthetic clothes cause the worst burns if it crashes. I also concentrate as hard as I can during the flight, to help the plane stay in the air, and if I can afford it I buy a bottle of perfume before boarding, because obviously we're less likely to crash if I've just spent twenty-five pounds on perfume. The one I got at Heathrow was Chance – which now strikes me as a bit ominous. Chance is not my favourite thing in the world. If they made a perfume called Security or Certainty, now, I would definitely wear that. I'd spray it all over.

Thankfully, Ed finishes his call without the car crashing. This time, anyway.

'OK back there, boys?' he asks over his shoulder.

Henry and Josh don't reply; they're plugged into their iPads, pinging and killing things on their screens. They each have an iPad and they're eight. It's insane. If

4

only my phone hadn't treacherously died on the plane, I would be listening to one of my audiobooks right now, instead of staring out at this unending string of chalets, hotels and snowy, darkening fields. We keep passing red LED signs with mysterious maps and numbers. I'd like to know what they are, but I can't ask Ed, because although he's officially my stepfather, he still feels like a stranger.

'What are all those numbers, Ed?' Mum asks. It's spooky how sometimes our thoughts run along the exact same wavelength. At other times, it's like she's from a galaxy far, far away.

'They show which runs are open and the snow depths at the top. So that run, near St Anton, has a hundred and fifty centimetres of snow at the top.'

'Fantastic!' says Mum in an experienced tone, as if she's been skiing every winter all her life.

Ed laughs. 'Not really, Siobhan. It's pretty average. But I'm glad you're excited.'

This is one of the things I don't like about him. Any time Mum says something ditsy, he laughs as if he finds that cute – as if he likes her being dumber than him. Which she's not. Her only problem is that she's too adaptable. She's like a chameleon. For example, whenever she's with other Irish people she starts sounding way more Irish, which makes me want to die inside. And now she's married Ed, she's reinventing us as this sporty family that go skiing together at Easter.

But I don't want to be angry at Mum. Because she's

the only person in the car who actually wants me on this trip.

'No, Ed. She's too young,' I heard her say, one night in February when I'd come home from seeing a film with Emma.

I froze in the hallway, not wanting to eavesdrop but also wanting to know what exactly I was too young for. An arranged marriage? Being sent away to a Swiss finishing school? Actually I secretly like the idea of finishing school. In my head, it's like *The Sound of Music*, which is one of my favourite films – except without the Nazis.

My ex, Jack, also loves *The Sound of Music*, which in retrospect should have been a clue that we weren't meant to be. The signs were all there, but I don't think I twigged until the night he stayed over at my place while Mum was away. I was all set for a romantic evening in front of the fire but it petered out after a few kisses. Then the next morning I heard him singing 'Let It Go' in the shower and things sort of . . . clicked.

'I don't think it's too young,' Ed said. There was a pause, and then he continued, 'But it's up to you of course.'

'It's just, I know Juno: she says she'll be fine but she'd be terrified alone in the house for a week. And . . . I think it's important we do something as a family?' There was a question in her voice that broke my heart, and I was almost glad for her when he said, 'Sure.' But he didn't sound as if he meant it. Then she went on, 'Is it the money? I can contribute . . .'

'No, no. Don't worry about that side of it.' Another pause. 'Though it is a lot to shell out if she won't enjoy it.'

'You don't know that,' said Mum, sounding hurt.

'I know, babe. I'm sorry. Come here.' And then there was a noise that was ten times worse than the previous argument and made me tiptoe outside and walk round the block and come home again, this time giving them plenty of warning with slamming doors and jangling keys.

What I should have done was burst in and say that *of course* seventeen was old enough to stay home alone, if that was what Ed wanted. I mean, what's more frightening: staying home alone and getting some study done, or going on a holiday where I could genuinely end up breaking my neck and living out the rest of my days on a life-support machine? But when I suggested as much to Mum the next day I got one of her rare but genuine 'no's. So, I'm going skiing. And yes, I am going to try to enjoy it, instead of giving Ed another reason to think of me as an ungrateful brat.

Ed is one of the founders of a very, very famous smoothie empire. When he married Mum, my best friend Emma (who always looks on the bright side) said, 'You can have free smoothies every day!' I hate smoothies. Ed makes one every morning, and the noise of it is ear-splitting; the first time I heard it I thought the house was falling down. He also works from home twice a week and leaves Sky News running in the background all day. Believe me, the endless footage of war and terrorism is not relaxing.

I look at Mum in the front seat, where she's playing Candy Crush. Whenever I play games like that she sighs and talks about it rewiring my brain and giving me ADHD. I suppose she's only playing it because she can't read in the car. She's an obsessive reader, like me.

That's why I can't understand what she sees in someone like Ed. My dad teaches philosophy at Birkbeck College, and he's brilliant and witty and kind. Everyone loves him; he has six hundred friends on Facebook. He wears glasses, cardigans and cords, and he looks like a sort of handsome, balding Humpty Dumpty.

Ed, on the other hand, wears Ralph Lauren and Penguin polo shirts, Diesel jeans and Nike trainers, listens to cooler music than I do, and rides a Vespa scooter. Which is another fear to add to my list: that Mum will be killed while riding on Ed's scooter. He also owns – believe it or not – a skateboard. If there's anything creepier than a thirty-nine-year-old man skateboarding, I don't want to know what it is.

'So tomorrow,' Ed is saying to Mum, 'I thought you and I could try out a blue slope, while the kids do ski school?'

'Well – it depends what Juno wants,' says Mum. 'Ju? Do you want to do ski school or come out with us?'

'Um . . .' I hesitate. I know, from all my online research, that a blue slope is the least dangerous – or rather the second-least. The least lethal one is green, then it's blue, then red, and then black – although obviously I won't be going near any of those.

Before I can reply, Ed says, 'Sorry, Siobhan – you can't go on the blue slopes until you've done ski school, Juno. It's too risky.'

'Oh. OK.'

Good. I'll be much happier in a nice warm classroom. Mum's already gone mad spending hours at the weekend practising on the fake slope at Wembley. She offered to take me with her but I always had more important things to do, such as studying or examining my pores in the steamy bathroom mirror, and also I was hoping that the ski holiday wouldn't happen. Except it has, and in fact the car is slowing down and we seem to be arriving at our group of chalets.

Now, this is like something out of *The Sound of Music*. Two storeys high, built of yellow wood with lattices and cut-outs, eaves loaded with snow. It looks cosy, homey, welcoming. Just like the gingerbread house probably did to Hansel and Gretel, and look what happened to them.

The boys have abandoned their games now and are swiping at each other behind my head.

'Ow! Dad, Henry hit me,' says Josh.

'I did NOT! Josh pulled my hair, and he said my Skylanders were all rubbish!' Henry howls.

Mum glances back and says tentatively, 'Try and keep it down, boys. Your father's parking the car.'

They both look sulky. Josh repeats, in a 'nah-nah' voice, 'Your father's parking the car.' Henry, who always copies him, starts doing the same, kicking the back of Mum's seat.

'Joshua! Henry!' thunders Ed. 'That's enough!'

They're both instantly quiet. And I find myself with two opposite but equally strong feelings:

1. They are brats and I hate it when they're horrible to Mum.
2. I totally know how they feel.

We've parked now. I feel reluctant to leave the car, which feels like a cosy bubble.

As we get out, a big, noisy group of about eight girls and boys comes towards us from one of the chalets. Even from this distance I can tell they're the kind of posh, intimidating people I dread. They look like a gang of Jack Wills models or Made in Chelsea extras. One girl is in the middle of a story, waving a cigarette around and talking at the top of her voice. The others are talking over her and laughing. The girls are in tight jeans, snow boots and Puffa gilets, and the boys are wearing bulky sports jackets, scarves and jeans.

World War Three has broken out behind me. Josh is screaming about something that Henry did, or vice versa – it's hard to tell with all the yelling but it seems to involve David, who is Henry's teddy bear. Henry is officially too old to carry around a teddy bear, but he does it anyway. I almost wish I'd brought Mr Ted, my own ancient bear, who lives in a basket in my wardrobe and is brought out at very low moments.

Ed has gone into full-on United Nations mode, practically holding a tribunal to establish who did what and why. Mum thrusts David at me, saying, 'Juno, hold that, please.'

Perfect. As they stride by me, they all clock me, in my non-sporty long black coat and Converse, holding a teddy bear. One of the girls looks at me and says something that makes them all laugh. At me.

All except one of the boys, who's taller and broader than the others, with dark circles under his eyes and a sort of beard-slash-stubble thing going on. He smiles when he sees David, but then looks away as if he's thinking of something else. Then they've passed me by, leaving their voices and footsteps hanging behind them on the frosty air.

3

The inside of the chalet looks like something from a magazine article. It's all cosy, caramel-coloured wood, like a matchbox, with beams on the ceiling and soft lighting, deep sofas and a pale sheepskin rug. There's also a big roaring fire with . . . a girl standing in front of it? Have we stumbled into someone else's chalet by mistake?

'Hello, my name's Tara. It's great to meet you!' she says enthusiastically. 'And this must be Henry? Or Josh?' She squats down to shake their hands, like an energetic children's TV presenter. She's short and curvy in black shorts and shirt, her wavy blonde hair is tucked behind her ears and she's pretty in a sort of chipmunk-cheeked way. Of course; she must be the 'chalet host'.

'I'm Josh. That's Henry. We're eight,' says Josh, gazing up at her.

'The perfect age to start skiing!' she says to Mum and

Ed. 'I started then – ten years ago, and I've never looked back!'

When I heard the chalet came with a 'chalet host' I pictured a Heidi-type figure who might scurry in now and then to peel a few potatoes. But this girl is so professional: putting the finishing touches to the place settings, and pouring us Prosecco. It proves my theory, that eighteen is when you finally become grown up. I look at her admiringly, trying to pick up a few tips.

'Glass of Prosecco, Juno?' Ed asks, looking around for me.

'Oh – no thanks.' I don't like sparkling wine, and also I'm busy plugging my phone in. Thank God I remembered my plug adapter. That's the good thing about being a worrier; it makes you an extremely good packer.

'Have you eaten, or would you like to eat with us?' Mum asks Tara.

'Oh! That's very kind. I have eaten, but I normally serve dinner . . .' Tara says.

'I think we can manage,' says Mum. 'Why don't you go and take a break?'

'Are you sure? That's great,' Tara says, looking thrilled. 'Emergency contacts and Wi-Fi password are in that folder if you need them. Breakfast at eight OK? Full English?'

'Perfect,' says Mum, practically shooing her out of the door.

When Tara's gone, Ed says, 'That was sweet of you,

Siobhan, but she is paid to serve dinner, you know. There's no need to feel guilty. We don't want her taking the—' he glances at the boys, 'taking advantage.'

'Come on, Ed. This isn't Downton Abbey,' says Mum, wrinkling her nose at him. 'Anyway, she looked too knackered to take advantage of anyone.'

Ed laughs, and I see that Mum's charmed him the way she's already charmed Tara. She's very good at it; part of her job is to charm money out of wealthy people to make them patrons of her theatre. That's how she met Ed, in fact. But Mum is also very thoughtful. I didn't even notice how tired Tara looked.

'You are a soft touch,' Ed says. He squeezes her close and kisses her, while I look away. Henry is sitting on the sofa, reading his Horrid Henry book with his mouth open, and clutching David. Josh is running around in circles, saying, 'Yes! There's Wi-Fi. Wi-Fi! Wi-Fi Wi-Fi Wi-Fi!'

I'm waiting for my emails to load. There's one from my ex, Jack. The subject line is: *Starbucks Boy – Major Breakthrough!!!* I skim through it, and learn that Starbucks Boy asked Jack what he was doing this weekend, which Jack reckons is a definite sign.

It's good to be friends with your ex, of course, and I want to support Jack, but sometimes I wish he'd involve me a bit less in his love life. He was my first proper relationship, and it's only been twelve weeks since we broke up. I'm not ready to hear how cute Starbucks Boy looks in his green apron.

Mum calls, 'Juno, come and eat. And no phones at the table.'

She looks happy and no wonder, with the fire roaring and the glasses sparkling in the candle light and her Brady Bunch fantasy all falling into place. Even the boys, for once, are eating quietly without making a drama about 'sauce' or the wrong foodstuffs touching each other.

'Gosh, this is a carb-fest, isn't it?' says Ed. 'Pie *with* potatoes.'

'I know, it's mad,' says Mum. 'And bread as well!'

I look at her sceptically, thinking: really? Have you really forgotten how much you used to love Dad's shepherd's pie with extra cheese on top? We used to eat normal things, like lasagne and chilli con carne; now we live almost exclusively on superfoods and things I can't pronounce, like quinoa.

'Is the Wi-Fi decent, Juno?' Ed asks.

'Wi-Fi!' says Josh happily under his breath.

'It's OK. I got online pretty easily.'

'Remember, though, Juno, no study,' Mum says quickly.

I nod, going red. I don't want Ed knowing what Ms Kelly the guidance counsellor said about me 'burning out', and overdoing things. The school librarian noticed that I was the first to arrive and the last to leave every day. Mum and Dad were called in for a special confab about it, and I'm under strict instructions not to do any study for at least a week. It's ridiculous, but it makes me feel so tragic and geeky, I haven't even told Emma about it yet.

Ed's phone buzzes, and he turns to Mum. 'Sorry. It's Simon again.'

'Don't worry!' she says, smiling.

'Don't worry ... be happy,' Henry sings under his breath, swirling his macaroni cheese in a lake of tomato ketchup. Henry is a dreamy kid: in a world of his own, with round glasses that add to the Harry Potter effect. He loves to reminisce about things that happened a few months ago, and often talks sadly about his old house – 'My beautiful house'. But he never mentions his mother, who died when the boys were five.

'Are we going to have tea at the adults' table every night?' asks Henry.

Ed says, 'Sometimes. Other times you'll eat earlier, or Tara will come in to babysit you.'

'We're NOT babies!' says Josh, putting down his fork and looking at his father sternly. Josh is the older by ten minutes but it might as well be ten years. I can totally see him as a grown-up, chairing board meetings and smoking cigars. Even his hair stands up assertively, unlike Henry's duckling fluff.

'Of course you're not babies! But Tara might come in, some nights, and watch *Ben 10* with you and Juno to keep you company while we go out.'

'Wait a second,' I say. 'You mean she can babysit the boys, right? Not me.'

To my shock and horror, Mum says, 'We'll see. I mean

you've never had them both; it's a lot of responsibility
... Tara could keep you all company.'

'Are you serious?' I say faintly. 'You're hiring *an
eighteen-year-old* to babysit me?'

'Juno, let's not decide right now, OK? We can talk
about it later.'

I'd love to make a scene and storm out, but where?
I barely know where I am and I don't even have any
euros. So I try to calm down, and remind myself that by
next week, the whole thing will be over and I can get on
with my normal life – what's left of it.

4

'What do you think, Juno?'

Mum's standing outside her bedroom, looking at herself in the mirror. She's dressed head to toe in her black-and-white skiing gear, with snowflake-patterned gloves. Mum normally wears vintage-style things – trailing dresses over heavy boots, or silk blouses and skinny jeans. Seeing her in sports gear seems wrong, like spotting an antelope on the beach.

'You look very nice,' I say truthfully.

Mum is properly beautiful, with blue eyes, dark hair, pale skin and high cheekbones. She trained as an actress, but she also had me to look after. I was born when she was twenty-one and she and Dad were students at Trinity College, Dublin. There's a photo of her and my dad at their college graduation, with caps and gowns and a bundle, which is me. She is the youngest of all my friends' mums by miles. Not that we ever get mistaken for sisters – I look more like my dad: strawberry-blonde hair down to my waist, green eyes, freckles and pale lashes which were the bane of my life until I turned fifteen and Mum took me to get them dyed.

'Why don't you have your gear on?' Mum asks.

'I don't need it this morning, do I? If I'm at ski school.' I don't know much about ski school but I presume it's like, well, school: lessons, desks, whiteboards.

'Juno!' says Mum. 'You're joking, aren't you? Ski school means group lessons, on the nursery slopes. *Surely* you knew that?'

'*What?*' I'm thunderstruck. 'No! I thought it meant school! Like in a classroom!' I know Mum's forbidden me from doing any study but I thought this would be an exception.

Ed appears behind Mum. 'What's this?' When Mum explains, he tries to hide a smile.

'We wouldn't take you all this way to put you in school,' Ed says. 'I mean, you get enough of that already, right?'

This is another irritating Ed-ism. Why does he always assume that I hate school? It's where my friends are, and I don't mind most of the teachers, and I want to do well. It's everything else that's a problem.

'Go and put on your gear, love,' Mum says quickly.

I shuffle off, unable to believe that I've been such an idiot. This whole place is messed up.

'Looks good! It all fits well, doesn't it?' Mum asks,

spinning me round, when I come back out in my ski gear, which is like hers but blue.

It does fit well for a death garment; except the whole thing is so obviously brand new I might as well have L-plates on. But that's the least of my worries. I'm so terrified about the prospect of doing actual skiing, I can barely swallow a slice of toast, let alone the cooked breakfast Tara is serving up. When the earthquake noise of Ed's smoothie starts, I nearly jump ten feet in the air.

'More coffee for anyone who wants it. Juno?' Tara asks.

'Oh, no thanks,' I say faintly. Coffee never tastes as good as it smells. Also, more nervous energy is not what I need.

Our chalet is on the edge of a cute Alpine village whose sole purpose of existence is skiing. Instead of newsagents, there are sports-gear shops, and instead of Starbucks there are fondue restaurants and cake shops. People are clanking around in giant boots, carrying skis and poles and wearing mirrored shades and Gore-Tex. I thought it would be cold because of the snow, but it's warm and sunny and I'm already too hot in my gear.

'Isn't this wonderful?' says Mum, putting on her sunglasses. 'The air's so fresh and clean after London . . . Smell the ozone, Juno!'

Ed laughs affectionately. 'I don't think you can smell ozone, Siobhan.'

'Yes, I know, Mr Pedantic,' she says, giving him a playful shove. He gives her a shove back, while I die a little inside. It's a sad day when your mother is more of a teenager in love than you are.

The ski-hire place is rammed with people measuring themselves against skis and trying on boots. Everyone's speaking German, and I start to panic again. How will I say 'Please call an ambulance' in German?

'Don't worry!' Tara says when I ask her. 'They all speak English and anyway, that's what I'm here for.'

I can't even get my ski-boots on, so Tara has to help me. They're the most uncomfortable things I've worn in my life, seemingly forcing my ankles back and forward at the same time. I can barely walk in them – how on earth am I meant to ski?

Once we've got our gear on, we clump off to a different place to register for our classes.

'I forgot how the first morning of skiing is mainly queuing,' says Ed, tapping his foot and looking longingly out of the window.

I'd queue all morning if it meant I didn't have to ski. I've noticed that Henry and Josh both have helmets, and I don't. Feeling four years old, I ask Tara again.

'They've run out, sorry. But you'll be fine, honestly. It's practically flat.'

I'm dubious about this, but she's already hurrying over to Ed. 'I'm terribly sorry. I'm afraid there's been a mix-up and the boys aren't booked in a kids' lesson for today. Would it be OK if they joined an adult beginners' class just for today?'

'That's totally fine – it'll do them some good,' says Ed,

and Tara's look of concern turns to relief. Ed is nice. I can admit that. So why do I not like him?

Tara brings us to the field where our class is meeting, and escapes quickly while Mum and Ed linger to say goodbye.

'Make sure you stay safe, love, OK?' she says anxiously. 'Don't take any risks.'

Finally Ed manages to drag her off to their own romantic ski session together. It's the first time I've been left alone with the twins, and I feel an odd sense of protectiveness. Under their helmets, their identical brown heads look very babyish. They don't even have poles, which seems wrong – just skis.

But the glimmerings of fond feelings towards them vanish when they start skedaddling towards the far side of the field, using their skis like snow shoes.

'Henry! Josh! Come back,' I call, helplessly. There's no way I can follow them.

'You're not in our club! This is the Space Ninjas' Death Ray Boys Only club!' Josh yells, turning round.

Little brats! Fortunately, a woman in the blue-and-white instructor uniform appears. She calls something at them in German.

'Oh, they won't understand – they only speak English. Their names are Henry and Josh,' I tell her.

'HENRY AND JOSH! RETURN HERE IMMEDIATELY!' she yells, clapping her hands. They stop dead, and start shuffling back towards us at once.

'Look, they're already learning cross-country ski,' says the instructor, whose name badge identifies her as Simone.

With the boys corralled back into the group, Simone gathers us for a quick introduction. There are two English couples in their twenties, a couple of older Austrian ladies, and a random Australian man in his fifties. We do a few drills together – learning to snowplough, which is like stopping in a V-shape – and everyone, including the twins, gets the hang of it quickly.

Except me. Simone keeps on having to interrupt the class to give me remedial attention. Eventually she moves on to more advanced moves with everyone else, while I stay in a corner attempting snowploughs. She also keeps calling me Yuno, which sounds vaguely Japanese and makes me feel even more conspicuous.

'OK, here's what we do next,' says Simone. 'We will try a gentle run up on the baby slopes – very, very gentle, Yuno.'

I'm not happy about this but I stumble along with the others towards the chair lift, where I'm buckled in with the two boys. They are deep in one of their mysterious conversations about superheroes. They don't even seem to notice that we're clanking high up into the sky. Far, far too high.

I'm too panicked to even figure out how to get out of the lift: Josh and Henry have to help me. And then we're standing at the top of a precipice with the rest of the group. It's crowded with other skiers, zipping past at top speed. There's no way I can make it down there without being run over. The boys must be terrified, too.

'Are you guys OK with this?' I ask them.

Henry doesn't say anything: he's making patterns in the snow with his ski. Josh says, 'It's fine.'

They're half my height and they're not scared. That means I have to do it. Now Simone's grouping us all to one side and making us all go one by one. Henry and Josh set off, whizzing down fearlessly like little clockwork toys. And I have to follow them.

Except I can't. My feet won't move. I'm clamping my poles rigidly to my sides and my legs are shaking. I can vaguely hear Simone in the distance; it sounds like a distant echo, as if I'm underwater. My heart is pounding so hard it feels like it's going to jump out of my chest and I'm finding it hard to catch my breath.

Next thing I know, someone's got me by the arm and has taken my poles, and I'm being led somewhere. My breathing's gradually coming back . . . and I see a toy train. A toy train with tiny kid-sized seats.

'Are you OK?' asks a voice. I turn round slowly.

It's the boy I noticed yesterday, the stubbly one, now wearing a blue-and-white instructor's uniform. He's looking at me with a mixture of pity and amusement.

Now, not only has he seen me arrive at the chalet clutching a teddy bear, he's helping me into a toy train.

'This will take you to a lift, which will take you back down to the bottom of the slope,' says the boy. He's English, and not as old as I thought. Nineteen? To calm myself down, I focus on how horrible his beard looks.

'Also, you should be more careful. Don't come out on the slopes again till you've had some lessons,' he says, in a judgey way.

Arrogant pig! I try to think of some kind of a comeback or put-down, but nothing comes out. He thumps the side of the train, which seems to be a signal for it to start, and I'm chugging off, in a kiddie ambulance. I'm just thankful that nobody seems to be filming me and that I'm not going to end up all over the internet as a vine.

Soon I'm limping along the path towards the place where we're meant to be meeting Mum and Ed. Maybe I can bribe Josh and Henry not to mention what happened.

But as I approach our meeting-point, I see it's too late for that. They all start exclaiming and pointing when I appear – all except Henry, who's singing one of his tuneless songs to himself. Mum is beside herself with anxiety.

'Juno! Finally!' she says. 'Josh and Henry said you disappeared with some man—'

'I sort of froze at the summit . . . I got a train down instead,' I explain.

'Oh, come on . . . summit?' says Ed, smiling. 'It's a very tiny slope.'

'Well, it wasn't,' I retort. 'It was really high, and I didn't know how to get down.'

Mum opens her mouth, presumably to tick me off,

then stops herself. 'How did that make you feel?' she asks earnestly.

This is a phrase she picked up in some article on how to parent teenagers. I know she means well but she doesn't understand how it works and she throws it at any minor setback – like when I burn my mouth on hot chocolate, or nobody retweets me.

'Terrified. I never want to go skiing again,' I say.

Now Mum looks disappointed. 'Oh, Juno,' she says. 'Come on. Really?'

Honestly. Why did she ask me if she didn't want to hear?

'Let's discuss it over lunch,' Ed says. 'I don't know about you, but I'm starving.'

5

We don't discuss anything over lunch, though, as it's taken up with Ed trying to persuade the boys to eat something other than chips.

'Look at him,' he says, nodding towards a French boy beside us in a pristine ski-suit. 'He's eating his delicious salad with no fuss.'

'That's because he's a loser,' says Josh. He makes the L sign on his forehead while Ed jumps to get him to stop before the French kid sees. As soon as that's died down, a fight breaks out over whether the boys will watch *Horrible Histories* or *Ben 10* this evening.

'We ALWAYS have to watch *Ben 10*. We NEVER get to watch my things,' says Henry in despair, and lays his head down on the table. Josh starts balancing the ketchup bottle on his brother's neck, and Henry swats it away, while Ed pries them apart.

Mum tries to weigh in. 'Why don't you watch an

episode of *Ben 10* first, and then a *Horrible Histories*?' she suggests.

'That's a stupid idea,' says Henry.

'HENRY!' says Ed. 'Don't talk like that to Siobhan. Say you're sorry.'

Henry reluctantly says sorry, and then Ed drags them both outside for some 'time out'.

'I'm sorry you had a bad experience skiing, darling,' Mum says to me. 'But if you'd at least give it another try—'

'I have tried it, and I hated it. All I want is to sit quietly in the chalet and read my book,' I explain. 'What's wrong with that?' I lean forward to eat a lukewarm chip from Henry's plate. Gross, but I deserve it after my traumatic morning.

'Nothing's wrong with it, Juno, except I think you would like skiing if you gave it a chance.'

'But why is it so important?'

'Because you spend too much time in front of a screen and studying – yes, stop making that face, it is possible. Skiing would de-stress you. It's sociable, healthy ... look at that gang over there. Don't they look as if they're having fun?'

It's the same people I saw last night. The boys and some of the girls are wearing the instructor uniform; they're all gathered around a table with rafts of Coke and a few beers, tucking into giant piles of fries and toasted sandwiches. And there's the one who put me in the toy train. He's got his back to me, but I recognise the width of his shoulders, and his shaggy mop of brown hair. They do look as if they're having fun: loud, suntanned, outdoorsy, posh, hard-drinking fun. The kind of fun that I'm completely allergic to.

'But that's not ... my kind of fun,' I say, trying to explain.

'But we're supposed to be having a holiday together – a shared experience.' She clasps her hands together to indicate the shared-ness of the experience.

'Mum. It's just skiing. It isn't going to magically make us a family.'

She looks so hurt that I instantly feel bad. We sip our hot chocolates in strained silence while I wonder whether to apologise – or stick to my guns.

'How about a private lesson?' she says eventually. 'Would you go for that? You could go at your own pace and see ...'

'Wouldn't that be expensive?'

'Well, don't worry about that.'

I know there's a lot more cash around now that Ed is in the picture, but it still makes me feel guilty. So guilty that I end up agreeing to a private lesson.

'If they do them, of course,' I add. If they don't, I'm off the hook.

'Of course they'll do them,' says Mum. 'Why don't you go over and ask them? Stretch your wings.' And she indicates the instructor gang.

'Ha, ha,' I reply, deadpan. When I was *much* younger, Mum sometimes liked to make me order something in a café or return something to a shop, to 'stretch my wings'. But that was when I was twelve. She can't be serious now. Can she?

'Of course I'm serious,' she says in answer to my question. 'Go over and ask them.'

I shake my head. She might have her 'no means no' face but so do I, and the idea of bouncing over to this group of *Made in Chelsea* extras calls for a definite no.

'Fine,' she says, exasperated. 'I'll ask them. Honestly, Juno, I'd like to see you grow up a little, I really would.'

'Mum! Don't!' I hiss. But it's too late; she's already threading her way through the crowded tables, ready to . . . Oh, the shame. The eight heads all swivel around, and stare at me before swivelling back at Mum. Now Toy Train is talking to her. He glances at me briefly. After a bit of chatting and nodding, Mum comes back over, looking very pleased with herself, while behind her the gang bursts out laughing.

'I can't believe you did that!' I whisper.

'Juno. Get over yourself. You're lucky to be having a private lesson. It's tomorrow morning at eight. With Boy.'

'Eight! That's so early!' Mum gives me another look and I drop it. 'What do you mean, Boy? What boy?'

'The big one with his hair all sticking up on end. It's a strange sort of a name, isn't it? I presume it's a nickname.'

Boy! What a ridiculous name. With his size and bearded shagginess, he reminds me of a wild animal.

Not a bear. He's too lean, more like a wolf. Wild Boy would be a better name. Or Wolf Boy.

But whatever kind of animal he is, he's not a friendly one and I don't want a lesson from him.

'What is it now, Juno?'

'Nothing, just—'

I'm tempted to tell Mum that I've already met him and didn't like him. But if I do, she's likely to either tell me to get over myself (again) or go up and have it out with him. So I keep quiet.

This is typical of Mum, though. She has a soft spot for oddballs. Crazy old men on the bus, random buskers – they're drawn to her, and vice versa.

'Why did you pick him in particular?' I ask.

'I didn't; he volunteered. He seemed keener than the others to earn more cash. Said he could fit you in before his other classes. So you'll have to make sure you're on time.'

'OK,' I mutter. Now any thoughts I might have had of cancelling are out, because he's relying on me. But then I see him stand up and stretch lazily, slapping one of the other guys on the shoulder as he does. He doesn't look like he relies on anything or anyone at all.

6

That evening, Tara serves up a three-course meal and eats with us as well, while the boys watch TV in a separate room. I thought I was a good cook, but she is a total pro. As she produces smoked salmon on brown bread, tarragon chicken with potato rosti (this is Austrian for 'shredded, fried, crispy and delicious') and then mint-chocolate pudding, I watch Mum and Ed join her fan club.

'Tara, this bread is fantastic,' he says. 'Did you make it yourself?'

'Yes, I did! I hope it's OK?' she asks anxiously.

'Amazing. Were you able to cook like this before you were a chalet host?'

'Oh God, no!' Tara laughs. 'I could barely chop an onion. I did a course.'

'Time well spent,' he says warmly. 'D'you want another glass of wine?'

He pours her out a glass, then Mum. He hasn't offered me one, and I know why. I've turned down his glasses of wine for months, and now he's sick of offering.

'So you've been here since the start of the season?' Mum says to Tara.

'Yes. I arrived in November, and I'm staying till the end of March. It's my gap year.'

'Where are you headed next year?' asks Ed.

'To Edinburgh, to study history,' says Tara.

'That's fantastic. You considered Edinburgh too, didn't you love?' Mum asks me.

'Yes, but UEA is better for English I think. Edinburgh is excellent, though,' I add quickly.

'What will you do once the season ends?' Ed asks, turning back to Tara.

'I'm going to go and work on an irrigation project in Kenya for three months,' Tara says.

'Where in Kenya?' asks Mum.

Tara says the name, which means nothing to me, and I bet nothing to Mum either.

'It must be quite isolated if they need wells?' Ed asks.

'Oh yeah, it is. It's 100 kilometres to the nearest town, and if you get sick it's a day's walk to a doctor,' she adds cheerfully. 'So I'd better not get sick, I suppose!'

I'm staring at Tara, trying to imagine her, with her cute chipmunky face, digging wells in a village in Kenya. I've only been on a plane once by myself, and that was to visit my granny in Cork.

'Aren't your parents worried?' Mum asks.

'No, no. They say I should go for it.'

At this Mum recoils, and I realise I can't imagine her saying 'go for it'. She's much more likely to say 'be careful'.

'Absolutely,' says Ed. 'You'll be fine. I taught English in a village in China on my gap year. Bit lonely, and I caught dengue fever, but I had the time of my life.'

'That sounds great!' says Tara. 'Apparently malaria's the one to watch for in Kenya.'

They swap enthusiastic notes on jabs and immunisation, while I ponder the irony that you have to be really rich to afford to go off and get those diseases.

'How about you, Juno? Are you taking a gap year?' asks Tara.

'I haven't decided yet. It depends on my results.'

The truth is, I don't want to take a gap year. Backpacking is my idea of a nightmare. I would be terrified of getting strangled or kidnapped or stumbling into a war zone. Also, it would be expensive and I don't want to rack up a load of extra debt before I even start studying.

'Where would you like to go? For uni, I mean?' Tara asks me.

'University of East Anglia, I hope. I want to study English. But it depends on my results.'

'Don't be silly – what can go wrong? Juno's been predicted three As, which is more than UEA require,' says Mum proudly.

'It's only a prediction, though,' I murmur. I don't add

that it was made before I got a stepfather and two very noisy stepbrothers.

I really hate it when she goes on about my grades. It reminds me of my first year in secondary school when I didn't realise that it was a bad idea to do too well in class, or put my hand up every time the teacher asked something. I didn't know any better, until my friend Mia told me that I had to stop. That was when I started to really learn – not the easy stuff, stuff in books, but how to pretend to be normal. It's different now, but I still live in dread of being told I'm showing off.

We've finished now, and Tara starts whipping plates off the table and clearing them away. I pick up a pile and take them into the kitchen, where she's loading the dishwasher.

'Oh, don't worry about that,' she says, scraping and sorting them at top speed. 'I'll do it. You go and chill out. The first day's skiing is always knackering.'

Wandering back into the sitting room, I find Mum and Ed kneeling in front of the fire, having one of their flirty 'arguments'.

'I'm telling you. It needs another log,' says Ed.

'No! It just needs a poke,' Mum says.

'You need a poke,' Ed says, prodding her, while Mum giggles and slaps him away.

Urgh. I tiptoe past them and escape upstairs where I do the best thing of the holiday so far: lie in the bath and read. My book's about a girl who lives in a huge bubble-dome following a crisis called the Shutdown.

Everyone in the bubble is in one giant group and there are no families. Mum has tried to stop me reading dystopian fiction as she thinks it makes me crazy, but frankly compared to this holiday, the scenario in my book is a dream come true.

7

Next morning is beautiful. The sky is intensely blue, the sun's bouncing off the snow, and my breath is sparkling white. I just wish I wasn't having a skiing lesson. I don't think it will be like *Step Up*, in which he teaches me hip hop and I teach him ballet and we both learn about life. I think this is going to be a humiliating episode in which an arrogant knuckle-dragger laughs at me while I do something very badly twenty times in a row.

I can see him now, leaning against the fence of the nursery slope. He's staring moodily into the distance and smoking. What a poser. I don't know anyone my age with half a brain who smokes. As I approach, he stubs out his cigarette and throws it on the ground. Littering: double gross! I look pointedly at the stub, but he doesn't seem to notice, just pushes himself away from the fence to stand upright.

'Juno? My name's Boy. B-O-Y, like the opposite of Girl.'

'I can spell Boy,' I mutter, leaning on my poles, and trying not to drop my skis.

He smiles. 'I'm sure you can, I just don't like being called Roy. Have you ever done any skiing before? Oh, wait a second. Have we met before?'

He doesn't even remember. I'm not sure whether to be annoyed or glad about that.

'I had one lesson yesterday. It didn't go so well.'

'Why's that?'

'Because . . . I hated it and I was awful at it?'

'Well, things can only get better then.' He yawns, without bothering to put a hand over his mouth, revealing a set of very white teeth. He really is a Wolf Boy. Rude Boy, also. I'm so annoyed at him yawning in my face, that I pick up the stub of his cigarette and hand it to him.

'I think you dropped something.'

He looks at me in astonishment before grinning again. 'Cheers,' he says, tucking it inside the pocket of his uniform. 'Now, put your skis on and face me.'

I can't even get the things on, especially with him watching me.

'Not that way. Step into the back of them first. That's it. Hang on to me if you want.' He holds out his arm, which I ignore. 'By the way, you really don't need that helmet.'

'I'm fine with the helmet, thanks.'

'Suit yourself. Follow me.' He clunks easily to the top of the field's gentle slope. While staggering after him, I manage to step on one of my own skis and nearly come crashing down on top of myself.

Boy just waits for me to get to my feet again and follow him. I'm already hot and sweaty, and deeply miserable, and I haven't even done any skiing yet. Why am I putting myself through this, again? Oh, now I remember. So that my mum can feel good about her new relationship.

'Now,' he says. 'Get comfortable on the skis.'

'Isn't that a contradiction in terms?' I say. 'Hang on. I forgot my sunscreen.'

'Really? It's eight a.m.'

Ignoring him, I slather on some sunscreen. 'I'm ready.'

'OK. Loosen your body, bend your knees. Stick your skis in an A-position like this. No, not a V, an—' But it's too late. I've already slid forward several feet, my skis have crossed again, and I've fallen over.

'That's good actually,' Boy says.

'What?' I look at him suspiciously.

'You've learned to fall. That's the first lesson. You've fallen and it's not so bad. Right?'

I shrug. I suppose he's right. It wasn't the end of the world.

'Now, let's try that again. Remember, A-shape. Copy me.'

I copy him and do my best to bend my knees and

lean forward. After sliding forward about three feet, I stop dead in alarm.

'Was that meant to happen?'

He looks amused, and gives me a thumbs-up. Now I definitely hate him. That was hard and he's acting like I'm a toddler who finished a Duplo tower.

'That was good. Well done. Now try it again.'

I have to admit, he is a good teacher. He's very patient, and notices what I'm doing wrong immediately and explains it clearly. Like Simone, he's also obsessed with me leaning forward: he mentions it about twenty million times. But unlike Simone he explains why.

'You're leaning backwards because you're trying not to fall,' he says. 'But if you lean forward and get into it . . . you won't fall.'

I try to do exactly that, but I hit something slippery, my skis go apart and I end up doing the splits and falling over. 'Ow!'

I've had enough. I'm cold, achy and miserable – and there are tears pricking at my eyes. If he sees me crying, I will literally – well, not want to kill myself because suicide is no joke, but I will want this snow to swallow me up.

Boy skis over and holds out a hand to help me up. His hand is warm, rough and big; it practically engulfs mine.

'That's enough for today. You did very well.'

'Not really,' I mutter.

'No, you did. Want to try one more time, so you end on a good note?'

I shake my head. I know it's cowardly, but I'm done. I can tell Mum that I've tried it, and it's not for me.

Now, for added awkwardness, I have to pay him. As he stuffs the crumpled euro notes in his pocket – the same pocket where the cigarette stub went – I notice that his nails are all bitten to shreds.

'Want another lesson tomorrow?' he asks. 'Same time?'

I shake my head. He looks surprised. I half-expect him to give me a talk about the joys of skiing, or the importance of not giving up, but he says, 'Walk around as much as you can, and have a sauna or a hot bath. It'll help with the stiffness tomorrow.'

'OK. Thank you.' Now I'm picturing him picturing me in the bath, and I'm going red. Tragic.

'No worries.' He steps out of his skis easily, and hoists them over his shoulder with his poles. 'If you change your mind you can ask at the office. I generally try to keep a slot free for private lessons,' he says. And then he clanks off without a backward glance.

Thank God that's over. I notice that, at the other corner of the nursery slope, an old lady with white hair and huge violet mittens is learning to snowplough. She's about ninety, and she's already far better than me. I'm obviously not one of life's skiers. I'm a Hufflepuff, an indoor cat, and that's all there is to it.

8

'So how was it?' Mum asks, when we gather for tea and cake and scones at the chalet. Ed, still in his ski gear, is rubbing in hand cream. Hand cream! My dad doesn't even use conditioner.

'Well . . .' I don't want to be whiny, but I do want to be clear. 'Not great. I kept falling over. I basically hated it, to be honest. But I've tried. So please can I not do it again?'

Mum sighs. Ed's finished creaming his hands now, and looks up. 'Did you not get on well?'

I shake my head.

'Oh well,' Ed says lightly. 'Early days. The boys had a good time, didn't you?' he asks them. The twins are lying upside down on the back of the sofa, still in their ski suits, looking at their iPads.

'Yeah,' Josh says absently. Henry doesn't say anything: he often lets Josh reply for him.

Nothing much happens for the rest of the evening. I try Skyping Emma, but our connection is rubbish.

'Hey! Can you hear me?' she asks, waving at the screen. I feel a pang of guilt as I see that she's been studying; there's a pile of books beside her and she's wearing her glasses and her favourite polka-dot onesie. Emma works extremely hard.

The connection drops so I go back to the sitting room, where the Wi-Fi's stronger, and try messaging her instead.

How was the lesson? she asks.

Hellacious. I ache all over. Trying to get out of doing it again. How are you?

There's a pause before she messages back, *I have NEWS!*

Ben news?? I message, Ben being the boy that she's liked ever since she met him at her art class.

The next message I get, though, isn't from Emma, it's from Jack. It says *OMFG. I just asked SB boy out. He said NO. Aaaaah.* Seconds later, another message comes in. *I CAN NEVER GO TO STARBUCKS AGAIN.* And then another, from Emma. *He is going to Ruby's party on Sat!! Should I go?? What do I wear? xx*

Wow. Nothing has happened for months in our lives and now I go away for three days and it all kicks off. I don't know who to reply to first. I'm so over-stimulated that I type out *That's amazing!! Wear your new red top xx*, and send it to Jack.

Jack messages back, *???*

'Juno, come to dinner. Leave your phone,' calls Mum.

'OK – hang on,' I say, quickly typing out to Jack, *Sorry! Wrong msg. Will talk soon.* I press send but it doesn't go.

'The internet's not working,' I say, looking up.

'Well, never mind. We're about to eat.'

'Mum, I'm just sending one message!'

'Come on, Ju, we're having a family dinner – OK?'

I bite my lip to stop myself saying what I'm sure she knows – that this is never going to be my family. I eat quietly, and then as soon as it's over, I get up from the table and put on my coat.

'Ju, where are you going?' Mum says.

'Out. I just want some air, so I'm going to a café. Is that allowed?' The real reason is I want to find somewhere with working internet, but I don't say that.

'Well—' she glances at Ed, which makes me even more annoyed. Why does she keep on asking for his opinion? It's none of his business. But he just says, 'Your call, Siobhan.' And then I'm annoyed that he doesn't care whether I'm here or not.

'Make sure you're back in an hour,' she says, trying to be firm but just sounding doubtful.

'OK. Fine,' I say, and step outside, closing the door gently behind me though I wish I could slam it.

9

Walking down the cutesy village street with its twinkling lights, I feel like one of those psychopaths who feel no emotion when they see flowers, puppies or kittens. Because, gorgeous as it is, I don't want to be here. It's like Ed's house – one of the beautiful terraced houses overlooking Highbury Fields. I remember walking past once and thinking that people who lived there couldn't have problems – not real ones. Then, three months ago, I moved into one of them.

I'd give anything to be back in my proper home, the one I grew up in. It's a tiny, messy, two-bedroom flat in the least fancy part of Camden, but it was cosy and comfortable. And Dad was there.

I need to find a café with internet access so I can message Jack and talk to Emma. The only place that's open but isn't blaring dance music is a bar called the Foxy Fox. I can't go in alone, can I? But, hovering on the threshold, I think of Dad saying 'What's the worst that could happen?' And I push the door open.

It's actually quite nice inside. Candles on the tables. A jukebox playing Abba. Near the bar, I spot a familiar pair of broad shoulders and a mop of hair silhouetted in the light. It's Boy. Instinctively I look around for the rest of his group before I see that he's *behind* the bar.

'Hi. What can I get you?' he asks briskly. He's wearing a stripy apron, but doesn't seem embarrassed about it.

'Um, hi,' I say distractedly. 'I need the Wi-Fi password, please. And I'll have a hot chocolate.'

'Here you go,' he says, sliding it across to me. 'Four euros, please.'

'Thanks.' I hand it over, thinking my allowance won't go far in this place. 'Um, can I have the Wi-Fi password please? I need the internet urgently.'

'Come on. Nobody ever *needs the internet urgently*,' he says, mimicking me. 'Unless you want the weather forecast? That I could understand.'

'Who cares about the weather forecast?' I reply, more rudely than I had intended. 'It's snowing. Or snowy.'

'You don't get it. The weather forecast is the most interesting thing on the . . . Hang on a sec. Here it is.'

He hands me a card with the password, and strolls over to serve a group of loud stag-party types on the other side of the bar.

As soon as I'm online, I start to calm down. Then I worry that maybe this means I'm an internet addict. Sipping my hot chocolate, I'm prepared to admit that it's a good one. It's creamy and rich and topped with marshmallows that are going stringy just the way I like them.

First, I contact Jack, telling him I'm sorry. Then I get a text from Mum: *Are you OK? What café are you in?*

I am not going to tell her that so she can come and collect me as if I'm twelve years old. *Not sure what it's called. Will be back in an hour.*

Then Jack messages me. *Please can we Skype? Am in hell xx*

Poor Jack! I Skype him right away.

'Hey Jude,' Jack says, when the connection comes up. He always calls me that. 'How's skiing? And what was all that about me wearing a red top?'

I decide that Jack's crisis gets priority over mine. 'Never mind – a mistake. What's happened?'

Jack pauses dramatically before saying, 'It's over with Starbucks Boy.'

This seems funny, considering it never began, but I don't say that. The upshot is: Jack asked SB out, SB said no and poor Jack is devastated. Jack could have dealt with it if SB had been straight, but he's heard from a reliable source – the head barista – that SB is gay.

'Oh no,' I say sympathetically. We analyse it from all possible angles and decide that Jack shouldn't be put off going into Starbucks again (after a decent interval) and shouldn't regret asking the guy out – because you should only regret the things you haven't done. (I'm not sure if I totally agree with this but never mind.)

'How's your mum?' I ask. 'Does she still want to go clubbing with you?'

When he first came out, Jack's mum said all the right things but *looked* very sad and kept on sighing and drinking too much white wine in the evenings. Now apparently she's changed her mind and is being uber supportive – too supportive, he thinks.

'She's been googling adoption agencies and telling me how I can "build a family"', he says. 'I can't tell her that for now I just want to fall in love. And get laid. OK, Mum! Coming! That was her. Can I call you back later?' And he's gone.

I thought I'd died and gone to heaven when I met Jack. Our school allows a tiny number of boys in the sixth form, and he was one of them. Not only was he one of the brightest people in our English class, he's charming and funny and a brilliant musician. I thought he was a dream come true. The dream part was true, anyway.

Still no word from Emma. My fingers hover over my phone as I write a text message to my dad. *I am sick of Ed. Can I live with you?*

But I don't send it. Dad is living in a one-bedroom flat above a corner shop in Camden, which is barely big enough for him, let alone for both of us. I should have said, at the time, that I wanted to live with him instead, but I was afraid of hurting Mum's feelings.

I feel so homesick for my dad. I wish I was in his flat, with piles of newspapers everywhere, him in his cardigan with holes in the elbows, sticking a pizza in the oven – Dad couldn't name a superfood to save his life. I would love to Skype him right now, but if I do I'll start getting upset and he'll feel bad. So I erase my message and send him a different one. *Greetings from Planet Ski. It turns out I don't like skiing. See you soon. Jxx*

Then I look briefly at the news. There's a story about a murder. I know that it's just going to upset me and I shouldn't click on it, but I do, and then I read another one about antibiotic-resistant superbugs, until I have to take a few deep breaths to calm down. Honestly. It's seventy-five days until my A levels. How am I going to cope if I can't even read an article about antibiotics without freaking out?

I'm distracted by a loud group of guys at the other end of the bar – one of them is downing a drink while the others yell 'Chug! Chug! Chug!' It's a bit much, if you ask me, especially since the rest of the bar is so quiet. I think the barmaid feels the same because she says something to Boy. He glances over his shoulder at them and says, 'Guys, take it easy please.'

He sounds totally relaxed – as if he's just told off a cat for climbing on the table. And they don't even question him, even though there's six of them and only one of him. There's a bit of eye-rolling but they're instantly quiet. He's a big guy, of course. But it's not that; it's the fact that he sounds ... not confident ... fearless. I've never heard anyone – not a parent, definitely not a teacher – sound so fearless. Must be nice.

10

Dad and I texted back and forth on my way home, and he encouraged me to give skiing one last try. So I'm back at the baby slope the next morning at eleven, meeting Isabel, my new instructor.

Isabel is Austrian, with blonde hair, sallow skin and a small friendly face with bright brown eyes. She's about Mum's age, which is reassuring. It must be possible to ski for a few years without dying or breaking your neck.

'So what did you do yesterday, in your lesson?' she asks, as we clump together to the top of the field.

'We did snowploughs . . . and I skied, I suppose, but slowly.'

Isabel asks me to show her my snowplough, and then together we practise skiing slowly down the same diagonal line Boy and I did together. I'm still thinking about Mum and Ed and Dad. I'm so distracted, in fact, that I forget to be worried about the skiing. In fact I'm almost daring something bad to happen because it will take my mind off my other problems. So I lean forward and throw myself into it, and suddenly . . . I seem to be skiing.

'Was that it?' I ask Isabel, astonished.

'Yeah, that's it! Let's try again. Back to the top.'

I realise it's a baby slope, and I'm probably going very slowly – but I know I've got it. When I come to a halt at the bottom of the field I'm beaming.

'Excellent!' says Isabel, clapping.

I manage it again, and then she starts teaching me how to turn. It's a little harder and I fall once or twice – but I'm skiing! I can do it!

I'm still raring to go when Isabel looks at her watch and says, 'That's it for today. You did really good!'

'Thanks!' I walk away feeling strangely elated.

It's funny how all you need is one thing to go right and it can change your mood completely. This time yesterday I was curled up on my bed, miserable and lonely and achy. But now, I'm . . . happy. Maybe it's the sun, or the blue sky, or the happy, healthy outdoorsiness of skiing, but I'm feeling positively bouncy. I'm not worrying about Ed or Mum or Dad. I'm not even worrying about my A levels.

As I walk, I listen to the crunch and squeak of snow under my feet. I look up and see ridges of fir trees on the lower foothills, white peaks above them touching blue skies. Everything is bathed in this crystal light that's as different from the air in London as champagne is to murky pond water.

At that moment, my phone buzzes. First it tells me there are seventy-four days to the start of A levels. Then I see a tweet from Scarlett Adams, who's in my year. 'English essay going SO badly – worst ever! #stressed #fail.' And a load of crying faces.

Immediately my blood pressure soars. Scarlett is forever tweeting about how little work she's done and how stressed she is, and then she gets all As. She was genetically engineered to succeed; her parents deliberately had her in October so that she would be among the oldest in her year. She also went around for weeks saying that nobody ever got unconditional offers from universities, and that you had to be a total genius to get one. And then she got an unconditional offer from Birmingham.

I know what I'll do. I'll go home, have a shower, make myself lunch, and then read the past exam papers I brought. When I say 'brought', I may have actually smuggled them in the bottom of my suitcase. I know I promised Mum, but one day of revision won't hurt.

At least that's the plan until I get home and find Tara crying in our kitchen.

11

When she hears me, Tara screams and drops a bottle of Ed's favourite whisky, which she had lifted to wipe the counter. It smashes, obviously, and so she runs for a mop, still crying, while I help her pick up bits of glass.

'I'm sorry about that!' Tara keeps saying as she scrubs frantically at the stone-tiled floor. 'I'll replace it! Please don't tell your parents!'

'Of course I won't tell them. But ... what's wrong?' I ask, looking around. The kitchen looks like the proverbial bomb site. There are floury containers everywhere and the sink's piled high with dirty dishes.

Tara tears up again. 'The dishwasher's flooded – I spent the whole morning mopping the floor and trying to get hold of the resort manager, and they can't send anyone to fix it till this afternoon. So now I have to wash up everything by hand, and I still haven't made the cakes for afternoon tea, and I've run out of butter, and I have to wait in for the dishwasher man and then on top of all that I'm meant to be doing another afternoon tea *and* dinner, at the Chalet Birgitte.'

'What? Why?'

'Because SJ who works there is sick. She ate a bad oyster.' Tara puts her face in her hands. 'And I'm so tired. I haven't slept for more than five hours a night. I'm sharing a room with three other girls and they snore, and hang their ski socks and bras everywhere and wake me up with their hairdryers and step on my head when they get down from the top bunk. All I can fantasise about is a room of my own, and a week to sleep.'

I'm stunned. She seemed so sunny and capable, off to dig wells in the Third World – I'd never have imagined she'd have such a meltdown. I pat her on the shoulder for a minute before I realise she needs more practical help. Washing up seems like a good place to start, so I pick up the biggest dishes and start running hot water and Pixie washing liquid over them. I must take a picture of that for Emma; she loves foreign stuff with weird brand names.

'What are you doing?' Tara asks.

I turn round. 'I'm helping! I'll wash up while you make cakes.'

'No, no, I can't let you do that,' she says distractedly. 'You're a guest.'

Now I'm annoyed. It's one thing for my mum, or even Ed, to treat me like a kid, but for this girl to start telling me what I can and can't do . . . As I crash dishes around I reply, 'Look, I'm perfectly capable of doing some washing up, you know. I'm seventeen, not seven. I could probably even make a cake or two if I had to. And make dinner!'

Tara looks at me with round eyes. 'OK! Thanks! If you're – I'll – great.'

She runs out to buy butter, while I finish washing up. There's a lot to do; I keep finding more shards of glass everywhere and the sink is clogged with the boys' cereal. But it feels good to be helping out. I used to do loads in our old place but Ed has a cleaner who comes twice a week (twice!) so except for unloading the dishwasher now and then, it's a while since I've been any use at all.

By two o'clock our chalet is sparkling, Tara's stopped hyperventilating and we're sitting down for a quick lunch of leftovers.

I've also discovered lots about her that's very interesting. For example, she's from Avebury in Wiltshire and lost her virginity under the stone circle there, she thinks her main fault is that she's too hard on herself, and she misses her horse Pepsi way more than she misses her parents. I think she was joking about that, though.

'You must think I'm pathetic,' she says, squeezing out the mop. 'Crying over a broken dishwasher.'

'No, of course not! Do you want a cup of tea?' I ask,

getting up to put the kettle on. To my horror, her eyes start filling up again.

'I'm sorry! That was weird. It's just so long since anyone made me a cup of tea,' she says, wiping her eyes briskly. 'I haven't had a night off in ten days, and it was meant to be tonight, but instead I'm going to have to serve dinner at SJ's. There's twelve of them, and they're big boozers. It's going to be hell. I wish she'd never seen that oyster. What was she even doing with an oyster? We're miles from the sea.'

Poor Tara. I did want to do some revision, but she looks so miserable.

'Maybe I could come and help you?' I offer.

'Oh!' She looks at me hopefully. 'Would you? I don't know if I'd be allowed . . . I mean you're a guest. No. I couldn't.'

'Why not? You could just sneak me in, couldn't you?' I'm quite shocked at myself suggesting this, but Tara's eyes light up.

'Yes! Oh – except, then you wouldn't get paid, would you?'

'Probably not,' I agree, though actually I've no idea. I hadn't even thought of getting paid, but now that she's mentioned it, it sounds like a great idea. I've never had an actual job, aside from babysitting, which is ridiculous.

'I know. Why don't I ask Gus? He's the resort manager. He's nice – he might say yes. They do have temporary staff sometimes.'

Tara gets on the phone to Gus, and even before she hangs up, I can tell from her smile that it's a yes. 'Yes!' she says. 'Thank you SO much. I can't believe you're doing this! I'm so happy. Um, I may not have completely mentioned that you're a guest in my chalet. I don't think he would like that.'

'That's fine,' I say, hoping it will be.

'Oh,' she says suddenly. 'I just thought of something. How do we explain it to your parents?'

'They're not my parents,' I say automatically. 'I mean my mum is, but Ed is my stepfather. They won't care. At least, I don't think they will.'

'Good. So if I show you where the chalet is, are you OK to turn up at six? I'll find you a uniform. Size ten, right?'

'Right,' I say, wondering what Mum will think of my new career. And whether I'm actually going to be able to carry this off.

12

'Now the great thing about this place,' says Tara, 'is that the kitchen is separate from the dining room. So no one can hear you scream.'

As I wipe my forehead with the back of my hand, I know what she means. Tara presses her hands to her face. 'It's already seven thirty! We've got about fifteen minutes before they start to get hangry. Where's the sieve?'

'Um – I think it's in the sink, under those saucepans,' I say.

Here's the thing about cooking: everything gets into everything else. All the surfaces are covered with butter, onion peel, wrappings of stock cubes and who knows what. My black uniform shorts are covered with flour, my eyes are weeping from chopping a billion onions, and I've used up a whole kitchen roll wiping my hands. I'm also so paranoid about dropping hairs in the food that I did a French plait, which is killing my scalp.

'How is that soup going?' Tara asks. 'Is it hot yet?'

'Fine I think,' I say, stirring the cream of chicken soup Tara made earlier. 'Except – do you think there's enough? The recipe said it was for twelve, but . . .'

'Eek. Twelve mice, maybe. We'll have to add some chicken stock.'

'We could also sprinkle some parsley on top,' I suggest.

'That's genius!' Tara says. She rummages in the cupboard. 'They only have beef stock, not chicken. Do you think that'll matter?'

'Um . . .' Personally I think it might taste weird but when I see the desperation in her eyes, I decide not to say so. 'It'll be great!'

Tara boils the kettle while I hunt for the scissors. That's the other thing about cooking: you spend most of your time looking for things. Finally, after finding the scissors on top of the fridge, I rush over to chop parsley over the soup. It's only when I put the packet back in the fridge that I notice it was coriander, not parsley. I've also noticed too late that the scissors had bacon fat on them.

'Great. Now, after the soup, they're all having roast beef, mash and gravy, except one who doesn't eat red meat who's having a mushroom pie, and then for dessert it's sticky toffee pudding for ten, and one nut allergy, so he's having ice-cream. Oh, and there's one who doesn't eat dairy, so she's having the pudding without ice-cream.'

'Got it,' I say uncertainly. 'Wait a second. Does the one who doesn't eat dairy know that there's dairy in the soup?'

'What dairy?' says Tara, as a tall, curly-haired man in a cowl-neck jumper comes in.

'Hello lovey!' he says to Tara, and kisses her on both cheeks. They chat for a few minutes about skiing, before Tara introduces me and I get the two-kiss treatment too. I presume it's just a social call, until he rubs his hands together and says 'We're ready for dins!'

'Aces!' Tara beams. 'Give us half a mo!' As soon as he's left, she mutters, 'Aagh! There aren't enough spoons.' She grabs a handful out of the dishwasher and starts washing them by hand, while I dry them. 'What was that you were saying about dairy?'

'Nothing, just . . . is she allergic or does she just not like it?'

'Detoxing. Why?'

'Nothing.' I decide not to mention the cream in the soup.

We each take a tray full of bowls. Tara quickly hands out chicken-and-beef soup with coriander and bacon fat – or as we're calling it, cream of chicken soup – and tops up everyone's wine. I forgot to bring the tongs for the bread rolls, so I distribute them with my fingers, but thankfully it's dark and the wine is flowing so no one seems to notice.

No matter how quickly we wash up, there doesn't seem to be enough space for anything. Tara's Nigella book is propped behind the gas hob, and we've had to put the pans of boiled potatoes on the floor to mash them. And everything takes longer than you think. We're kneeling and bashing helplessly at the pans and sending potato shrapnel flying, but they still won't mash.

'Let's add more butter,' Tara suggests. 'That's the answer to everything.'

We're about to clear away the first course when Tara remembers about heating up the gravy.

'I'll put it on a low heat, and we'll go and get the soup bowls, and by the time we come back it'll all be done,' she says, and we run upstairs with the trays.

'The soup tasted interesting,' one guy with a very red face says. 'Was it a fusion recipe?'

'Yes! Alpine fusion,' Tara says, madly. Everyone applauds as we take all the bowls away.

'Do they normally clap?' I ask Tara, as she pushes the swing door to the kitchen open with her bum.

'Only when they're drunk,' she says. 'Right. Let's clear some space over here and plate up.'

We've got about half the beef and mashed potato ready to serve when Tara looks up at me, frowning.

'What's that smell?' she asks.

'I don't know. It's weird, isn't it? Kind of like burning . . . Oh, no! Look!'

Flames are leaping merrily from behind the cooker. Tara's cookbook is on fire.

'Nigella!' Tara shrieks. She rushes to rescue the book, and whirls it around before chucking it in the sink, while I turn the heat off and open the window.

'Can you imagine what would have happened if we hadn't come down? The whole chalet would have caught fire!'

We both look at each other in horror while I picture the whole place in flames. But then Tara starts giggling and within seconds, I'm laughing hysterically too.

'At least the book survived, except for the cover. Oh no!' Tara says.

'What?'

'There are burned bits of Nigella all over the gravy.' She shows me the pan with the gravy flecked with bits of charred paper. We look at each other in dismay. There's no way we can pick all those scraps out.

'What you don't know doesn't hurt you, right?' She stirs it around so the burned bits disappear into the gravy, and we carry everything out to the guests.

Back in the kitchen, Tara knocks back half a glass of red wine and immediately pulls on her washing-up gloves. 'Right. One more push, then it's pudding and done.'

By the time we've served pudding, it's nine thirty. I've just finished running the dishwasher for the second time. We unload it, nearly dead with exhaustion. Tara suggests a coffee, which I drink obediently: I need some kind of stimulant. Finally, with every muscle aching, we put the last clean plate away and wipe the counter down.

'We did it!' Tara says, high-fiving me. 'Now let's get out of these uniforms and straight to the pub.'

'The pub? I thought . . . didn't you want to go home and sleep?'

'I'm too wired to sleep. What do you reckon? Oh and before I forget – your wages! Gus said for me to pay you cash, and he'll settle up with me later.' And she hands me forty euros. Forty euros, for four hours' work. Not bad!

'So are you coming?'

In for a penny, I decide. 'Sure!'

13

The Tavern is rowdy and packed with guys wearing woolly hats, Puffa jackets and fleeces; there's even a group of men dressed as bears. Christina Aguilera is singing loudly about how she's going to feel the moment. Tara seems totally revived, and charges to the bar. I'd like to buy her a drink but according to the Austrian laws, I can only buy wine and beer, not spirits. (I looked this up before I came, obviously.)

'Oh don't worry,' says Tara. 'They won't ask for ID here. But I'll get this. What do you want?' she yells.

'Bailey's with ice, please?' I say, hoping that the fact that I can name a drink makes me sound sophisticated. I offer to pay, but Tara waves it away.

'You saved my life, I can buy you a drink. Cheers!'

'Cheers!' I take a sip and stare at all the sporty, happy after-skiers. Just when I'm thinking I must look like them, I spot my reflection. My face is so red it's clashing with my hair and my French plait is unravelling. I would undo it but I'm paranoid that my hair still smells of onions.

'Oh look there's Lara. Lara!' yells Tara.

Lara, shouldering her way to us through the crowds, turns out to be Tara's friend, even though she's quite a bit older – in her mid-twenties at least.

'This is Juno!' Tara shrieks.

'Hi Judo!' says Lara. 'What are you drinking, pig-face?' she asks Tara.

'Duh. Jagerboos!' And they high-five each other while I try to look as if this is all normal. I suppose it must be.

Lara orders a second round of Jagerbombs, and starts firing a load of questions at me. I'm a little intimidated.

'So how did Tara rope you into this? Are you a new chalet host, or what?'

'No, I'm a guest. In Tara's chalet.'

Lara's jaw drops.

'I know. Best guest ever,' Tara grins.

'Well cheers to you! I have never heard of a guest doing something like that.' Lara looks positively admiring. 'What's your skiing like?'

'Not great,' I admit. 'I've had a couple of lessons.'

'With who?'

'One with Isabel, and one with a guy called, um, Boy?'

'The Gruffalo!' says Lara. 'Look, he's over there.'

I turn round and see that Boy is sitting on the other side of the bar with his usual gang. They're all looking at their phones and flipping their hair around. Boy's the only one without a phone, and he seems bored.

'Some people think he's hot,' says Lara. I'm puzzled for a minute before I realise she means Boy.

'Not me,' says Tara. 'He always looks grubby to me.'

'But he's not bad as instructors go.' Lara turns to me. 'Some of them think they're gods. Especially the snowboarders – they're the worst—'

'But Boy is weird, he's not like the normal instructors,' Tara interrupts Lara. 'He hangs around with that crowd of Ra-heads and ski princesses, but he's obsessed with saving money. He lives off stuff that's nearly expired.'

'Yes! And he lives in a weird room above some garage; it's not properly heated or anything. Oh, and he works some nights in the Foxy Fox, doesn't he? I've never heard of an instructor doing that.'

Tara starts telling Lara all about our disaster-dinner, and they swap horror stories of twelve-hour shifts and going through bins to find a guest's false teeth.

'But the worst thing is I've put on so much weight,' moans Lara. 'I've got a serious case of BCGB. Big Chalet Girl Bum,' she adds to me.

'No, you haven't. I've become a whale,' says Tara.

'If you're a whale what does that make me? I'm, like, a brontosaurus,' says Lara.

I giggle and yawn, and realise I'm knackered. Also, my hair does smell terrible and I'm not sure how well my deodorant is holding up. I think I need to go home.

'Thanks again!' Tara says, and gives me a big hug.

'Oh, wait. Are you going to be OK walking home by yourself?'

'Why – oh.' That's a good point. Mum had to give me a lift to the chalet where we made dinner. It was only five minutes' drive but that's a long walk. And it's dark. 'I suppose I could call Mum and Ed. But I imagine they've both had a few glasses of wine by now. It's fine. I'll walk.'

But Lara is having none of it. In spite of her Dudes and Jagerbombs I think she's actually quite protective.

'I know,' she says. 'Your chalet is right by Boy's creepy garage – why don't you ask him to walk with you? He looks like he's leaving.'

It's true. Boy is standing up and has his battered green parka on. With its fur-lined hood, it makes him look even more wolf-like.

'No, no, no,' I say, horrified.

'Don't be silly. I'll ask him,' says Lara.

'No!' I shriek. But it's too late; just like Mum yesterday, she marches up to Boy.

'I'm so embarrassed,' I mutter to Tara. 'He'll think I asked her to do this.'

'Who cares?' says Tara. 'It's dark out. He can walk you.'

Maybe she's right. But then I see Boy, slinking behind Lara, hands stuffed in his pockets. He looks like someone who's been told to walk his sister to school.

'You ready?' he asks, looking into the distance six inches above my head.

I feel totally humiliated. I shouldn't care what he

thinks but I also know that if I was one of his cool gang, or looked like Mila Kunis, he'd be a lot more enthusiastic about walking me home.

'Bye!' Lara and Tara say, hugging me like a second set of parents. Just when I thought it couldn't get any more embarrassing, Tara calls after me, 'Text when you get home!'

14

We push our way outside through the heaving bodies, made ten times bigger with their Puffa coats and fleeces. I'm just thinking how nice the fresh air is, when Boy stops to light a cigarette.

'Look. Just so you know – I didn't ask Lara to ask you to walk with me,' I say awkwardly.

'Oh, I know you didn't. Don't worry, I'm not *that* dangerous.'

'No, no! I didn't mean it that way. Just – they were being over-protective.'

'Sure,' he says, as if it's not worth arguing with me.

We step off the porch and walk in strained silence. I send Mum a quick text: *On way home. See you soon.* I'm using a template because I've sent that message so often. Will I still be texting her that I'm on the way home when I'm forty? Probably.

We're on a deserted lane now: just firs and snow, and

long dark gaps between streetlamps. I feel spooked. Maybe he *is* going to murder me and make it look like a suicide? Or worse? I feel in my pocket for my phone, trying to plan what I'll do if he grabs me.

'Are you sure this is the right way?' I ask doubtfully.

'Yeah, it's a short-cut. Why?'

'Nothing, just – it's so quiet. It's like a horror film.'

He laughs. 'You obviously haven't seen many horror films.'

I no longer fear that he's going to murder-suicide me. He's just going to patronise me to death.

'No, I haven't,' I say coolly. 'I don't like them.'

'Neither do I,' he agrees, unexpectedly. 'I prefer to be scared in real life.'

'You *like* being scared,' I repeat. Obviously he's just showing off, but still.

'Of course! It's the best feeling in the world – going down a black slope or diving off a cliff, riding a horse or a motorbike . . . even climbing a roof will do.'

'Don't you think the real world is frightening enough?'

'How come?'

I turn to gaze at him. 'How *come*? Take your pick. Looming global crisis due to climate change. War and terrorism all over the Middle East. Not to mention a shrinking economy, increasing inequality, and we'll all have to work until we're ninety and have no pensions – and that's if we ever get a job.'

I break off, wishing I hadn't said all that. Most people

think I'm a total freak when I come out with this sort of thing. If they're kind like Emma they tell me everything will be OK. Or if they're Mum, they look worried and talk about limiting my internet time. But people can also get angry when you mention stuff they don't want to think about, so I tend to say nothing.

Boy's quiet for a minute before he replies, 'On the other hand, this guy who's a double amputee has just learned to control two prosthetic arms – by using his mind. It's called brain-interface technology and it could change people's lives.'

He goes on at some length about the technical details of the arm and how it's constructed, demonstrating by moving his own arm around. He goes into so much detail in fact that my eyes glaze over, but I do appreciate that – in his own weird way – he's trying.

'Also,' he continues, 'did you know, battery cages for hens were banned in the EU in 2012? That's good news, if you're a hen.'

'Oh,' I say, surprised. 'I never heard about that. How did you know?'

'Heard it on the radio. And I was designing some hen coops at the time, so I was interested,' is the unexpected reply. 'And crime in the UK is at its lowest level since, I'm not sure, the 1980s or something.'

'Is it? No. It can't be!'

'It's true. If you ask people they always say crime's on the rise, but it's actually dropped. So's smoking.' He grins at me, waving his cigarette.

I smile back slowly, amazed. It's so long since I've heard any positive news – let alone all these little nuggets.

We've dropped down a hill and turned a corner; we're almost back at our place. Which is kind of a pity. I was enjoying talking to him.

'Here you are,' he says. 'It's this one, isn't it?'

'Yes, it is. How did you know?'

'Lara told me. I know the names of most of the chalets.'

'Oh. Well . . . Thanks for walking me home.' I want to add something about how I enjoyed our conversation, but I decide not to. I'm halfway up the stairs to the chalet when he says, 'Hey.'

I turn, wondering if he's going to say something nice. Stranger things have happened, right?

'You might find this useful another time,' Boy says. He hands me a card from his pocket. It's a local taxi driver.

'Oh. Thanks.' I hurry inside, glad that it's too dark for him to see me blush.

15

I wake next morning with a queasy feeling. Then I remember. Boy was forced to walk me home, and then gave me the card of a taxi driver so that he never has to do it again. I'm also a little hungover. I find myself craving Diet Coke at breakfast (not that I'd dare to drink that with Ed around – talk about a bad example for the boys). So it's hard to concentrate on Mum's million questions about dinner last night and how it went.

'How many people did you say there were?' she asks again.

'Twelve, Mum. I told you. Yes, I will have an egg actually. And some bacon. And is there any more toast?' I'm starving.

'But Tara must have done most of it, surely?' Mum asks. 'You've never cooked for such a big group.'

'No, we did it together. Juno was a total star!' Tara calls, from over by the stove.

'That's amazing, darling! I'm incredibly proud of you!' says Mum, which is nice of her but also just – embarrassing.

Ed nods. 'Good work.'

I smile at him, shyly. 'Thanks.'

'And how did you get home?' Mum says. 'One of us should have picked you up.'

'It was fine, Mum. It was, like, ten minutes. I walked.'

'Alone?'

'No, with one of . . . one of Tara's friends.' I think it's best not to say 'one of the instructors'.

'A girl or a boy?' Mum asks instantly.

Aaargh! It's as if she wants to get right inside my head and rummage around the contents like a kitchen drawer.

'Is there any coffee?' I ask, as a distraction.

'But you don't drink coffee!' Mum says.

'I do sometimes.' Ed passes me the metal cafetière full of rich, thick coffee. I add two sugars and lots of milk, and it's not bad at all.

After breakfast, I help clear the table, while Henry and Josh play a game together on one of the iPads. As usual, Henry seems to be getting a raw deal. He's practically squirming onto Josh's lap in his efforts to see the screen.

'Stop . . . Jooosh! It's my go!' he complains.

'Henry,' says Josh sweetly, 'I'm doing this *for both of us*.'

Mum looks taken aback when I ask if I can have

another private lesson with Isabel. I offer to put my whole forty euros towards it, but she says it's fine to give her twenty. She's so thrilled that I'm getting into skiing, she'd probably pay for ten lessons.

However, when I get to the office, it turns out that Isabel isn't free.

'The only person I've got . . .' The girl at the desk clicks on the screen in front of her '. . . is Boy, at twelve. Is that any good?'

'Oh. No. I mean . . . that's . . . a bit too early.' I don't want a lesson with Boy. He will definitely think that I'm stalking him. 'Do you have anyone – anything later?'

'Boy is also free at two. He's had a cancellation today.'

I make a lame excuse about how those two exact times don't suit, and trail out of the office. It's such a brisk, blue, sunny day, I actually *want* to be on the slopes, skiing – or trying to.

Wow. Who would ever have thought that I – the person who spent weeks hiding in the locker room reading P.G. Wodehouse during PE – would ever look forward to exercise?

Since I'm at a loose end, I go home and help Tara clean up from breakfast. She's almost finished, but seems pleased to see me anyway.

'So what happened with Boy?' she asks. 'He didn't drag you off in the bushes and murder you, did he?'

'No. He was just a bit weird.' I open up the dishwasher and start putting glasses away. I love unloading the dishwasher; everything feels sparkly clean and warm.

'It's a pity because I just went to the office to ask about a lesson, and he was the only one free.'

'So did you book him?'

'No. I don't want him to think I'm stalking him.'

'Oh,' says Tara. She starts wiping down the counter.

'What?'

'Nothing, just ... If there's one thing I've learned from working here, it's that you're not going to bond with everyone, but you can still get along somehow. He doesn't have to be your best friend, he just has to be able to teach you to ski.'

Hm. She makes a good point.

'But it's up to you. Hey, you should come out with us again tonight,' she adds. 'It's everyone's night off. I'm going to wear my pulling top.'

That sounds like fun, but I'm a little scared by the mention of Tara's pulling top. I don't own any pulling tops. What if it's a foam party or a topless bar?

'Thanks. I'll see how I feel . . .'

As soon as I've said this, I regret it. I'm being cowardly. Almost to compensate, I say, 'But maybe I will have a lesson with Boy. I'm never going to see him again after this week. So it doesn't really matter.'

16

'Hey,' says Boy, as I come to a halt at the bottom of the slope. 'That was great. You've come on a lot in two days.'

I'm about to say 'No way' or 'I'm still rubbish' when I remember how important it is for girls not to put themselves down or argue with compliments. Especially with someone who has a tendency to be patronising anyway. So I say, 'Thanks.'

He seems to be on his best behaviour today, I suppose because he's got his professional instructor hat on. And I'm actually doing pretty well. We're on a lovely gentle slope and, after a few scary moments, I find myself gliding along beside him like a total pro – at least, I'm not falling over.

'So, I was thinking,' he says, while we pause for a breather. 'You know you were talking about global Armageddon – rising tides, and the zombie apocalypse and all that?'

I look at him suspiciously, wondering if he's making fun of me. 'You mean climate change? What about it?'

'Well, what's your plan of action?'

'How do you mean? I don't have a plan of action.' I feel guilty now, because aside from worrying, and letting my hair dry naturally, I don't do much for the environment. 'I mean I recycle, and I walk everywhere or get the bus . . . And I shop in Oxfam. Sometimes.'

'I'm not talking about stuff like that. I mean survival skills. If you're really scared, you should make sure you know how to light a fire, purify water, make batteries, build a house—'

'Build a house? Really?' I say sceptically.

Of course, this isn't the first time I've worried about what skills I could use in a post-apocalyptic scenario. The answer is: none. I can't use a bow and arrow, or skin a rabbit. I can't even make a fire. I suppose I could take some kind of wilderness survival course, but that would be way too sensible. Also not very compatible with my A levels.

'You look unconvinced,' Boy says.

'I'm not . . . I was just thinking it's a pity I can't use a bow and arrow.'

'A gun would be better. Here's what I would do. Identify the nearest big supermarket well in advance, and when it all kicks off, get myself there with some guns, and take it over. I'd be able to live for months.' He looks pleased with himself, but I'm horrified.

'Take it over – you mean by shooting the other

hungry people? And what happens when the food runs out?'

He frowns, then laughs and says, 'Fair point. Let's have another go at those snowplough turns.'

So we work on my turns, and he's so patient that I decide to overlook his gang-lord survival plans. I'm surprised when he says our time is up.

'Thanks ... that was great,' I say awkwardly, as I hand him my sweaty euro notes, trying not to feel like Richard Gere in *Pretty Woman*.

'So – do you really think there's going to be an Armageddon soon?' he asks, pocketing the notes. 'Like, in the next ten years?'

It's hard to know how to reply to that.

'Not an Armageddon exactly, no. But climate change is happening, and it's already causing problems.'

'Go on.'

He seems serious, so I give him a couple of examples: droughts in California, and flooding in England, and resource wars in Egypt and Syria.

'Huh,' he says. 'You certainly know your stuff.'

'It's just from reading the news.' Then, worried that I'm being too depressing, I add, 'But we're not seeing it so much in Europe yet.'

'Depends who you ask,' Boy says. 'It seems like the season gets shorter every year, and they're using more and more artificial snow.' He shrugs. 'That's according to my landlord. But nobody listens to him. The resort managers say things like, "We've had a record snow year!"'

'That's because they don't understand the difference between—'

'Weather and climate. Exactly.' I'm surprised to find him nodding in agreement. I'm even more surprised when he says, 'Are you walking back into town?'

We walk back into the centre, fighting our way along the narrow stone pavements, past the usual stream of Austrians in full-length Puffas, English men in novelty skiing outfits, girls in skin-tight jeans and leggings and moon boots. A couple of girls check out Boy as he lumbers past. It's probably because of the instructor uniform, or because he's at least a head taller than everyone else.

'Hey!' he says suddenly, and crouches down to pick something up from the ground. 'Fifty cents, yes please.'

This makes me laugh because it's something my dad does. I would, too, if it weren't for the germs.

'It all adds up, you know,' he says.

'Sure. Sorry – what were you saying just then?'

'You were asking about my plans for the end of the season. I'm going to do some climbing.'

'Where?'

'Everest.'

'Oh!' What with Tara digging wells in Africa and Boy climbing Everest, I'm feeling like a total shut-in. 'Have you done training and stuff?'

'Yeah, I do a hike every weekend and some evenings as well. I did Mount Pumori last year – it's the summit beside Everest. But the weather was too bad, and we had to come down.'

'How was it?'

'It nearly killed me. It's not the climbing so much as the altitude sickness. I remember one time, vomiting up my anti-nausea tablet, and . . . yeah. I better not tell you the rest.' He smiles to himself.

'Did you swallow it back again?' I ask, and immediately wish I hadn't.

'Yep.'

How revolting. He laughs, and I notice again how white his teeth are against the tan and beard, and how his canine teeth are slightly pointed.

'But . . . people have died up there, haven't they? I saw a documentary about it.'

'Oh, that was K2. It's even more dangerous. But yeah, people do die on Everest. Or they turn back. One in four people who start doesn't reach the top.'

'When are you going?'

'I'm booked to start in June – I should be able to pay for it by then. The permit is ten thousand dollars.'

Oh, my God. Ten *thousand* dollars?

'That's a lot of money.'

'I know,' he says. 'But I'm nearly there. I've got nine thousand.'

No wonder he's scrabbling for coins. But still. There's a lot you could do with that kind of money – such as give it to charity, or spend it on university fees, or basically don't blow it all on a trip that might kill you.

Also: what about the environmental cost? He was just talking about global warming but he doesn't seem to care about his carbon footprint.

'What?' he says. 'You're looking kind of disapproving.'

'Am I? No I'm not.'

'Come on,' he says, grinning. 'Admit it. You think it's way too dangerous and I should stay safe on dry land . . . Am I right?'

It's not so much his words, but his patronising smile that makes me reply, 'Actually, no. I was thinking about how you're burning all that carbon to fly there – and helping to melt all the snow off Everest. Not to mention all the rubbish climbers leave behind up there.'

I close my mouth. I never lecture people on stuff like that – because who am I to talk? I'm just as much of a first-world monster as anyone. But he sounded so smug, I couldn't stop myself.

He doesn't look smug now; he looks really annoyed.

'First of all,' he says, 'I'm not going to leave any rubbish. And secondly, what does your dad's Mercedes run on? Cooking oil? Did you walk to the resort?'

That is out of order, and I'm so annoyed at him calling Ed my dad that I just say, 'Forget it. Thanks for the lesson.' And I cross over to the other side of the road. He stands there looking at me for a second, and I wonder if he's about to come after me and apologise, but of course he doesn't. He just stomps off in the other direction, while I decide that next time, I'll be joining a group lesson.

17

'If we go out for half an hour can you mind the boys?' Mum asks, as soon as I'm in the door. 'We just want to go and have a coffee.'

'OK – can I change first?' I wanted to do some revision, but I'm pleased that they're finally trusting me to look after the boys, even if it's only for half an hour.

I run upstairs for the world's quickest shower and change into tracksuit bottoms and my favourite giant Topshop jumper, and come downstairs to say goodbye to Mum and Ed. Then I join the boys, with the vague idea of suggesting a board game or something. But they're deep in their Horrid Henry books, and don't even look up at me. I wish I was one of those people who had an effortless 'way' with children – like Katy in *What Katy Did*. Then I'd be the heart of the household, and the boys would bring all their little troubles and joys to me.

But the boys aren't showing signs of bringing me any troubles or joys. In fact I barely know them. Partly because they're such a unit; they don't seem to need anyone else. But also, they're eight. What are you into when you're eight? I liked Harry Potter and glittery stickers. Whereas these two . . . who knows what they're into?

'Who's this guy?' I ask, picking up a blue plastic dragon beside me.

Henry looks up. 'Warnado!'

'Oh.' That doesn't really answer my question. 'Is he from a book, or . . .'

'Skylanders!' Henry says. He puts down his book and shuffles over. 'He's one of the Lightcore, so if you put him on the Portal of Power it flashes up and goes BOOM!' He mimes, staggering backwards and waving his arms.

'Cool. And um, where does he live?'

Henry stares at me as if I'm nuts and goes back to his description of Warnado. I lie down on the sheepskin rug, where I can listen to him comfortably, and bask in the fire. I decide that I will go out with Tara, if I can think of something to wear.

'I'm bored,' says Josh.

'Why don't you read your book?' I suggest.

'I finished it. Want to play chess?' says Josh.

'If you want, of course.'

I know how to play chess reasonably well – as in, I know what all the pieces do – and I'm prepared to be nice and let Josh win. But he beats me in about six moves. I stare at him in astonishment. He's eight! How did he learn to do that?

'You can be white this time,' he says kindly, putting all the pieces back for a new game.

This time I concentrate harder, and I last about eight moves until it's clear that I'm about to lose my queen.

Henry's put down his book and has come over to watch. 'You should castle,' he whispers loudly in my ear.

'How do I do that?'

'Henry, stop helping her!' says Josh fiercely.

'I wasn't helping her! I just said to castle and she doesn't even know how!'

Josh jumps up, pushes Henry away, and then puts him in a headlock.

'Oh, Josh, that's not nice,' I protest. 'Let him go! Or I'll have to tell your dad.'

But Henry, still in Josh's stranglehold, lifts his head and says, 'No! My poor brother!'

I can't help it. I start giggling. The boys are so surprised that Josh lets Henry go and they both stare at me.

'How's everything here?' says Ed, coming in with his coat still on. 'Are you two being good? Have they been all right?'

I pause just long enough to mess with their heads, and say, 'Yes, they have.'

'How was your day?' Josh asks, in a very polite way. I've heard him ask this before. He doesn't always listen to the answer but it's still quite sweet.

'It was good thanks, Josh. Run and get some carrot sticks, and we'll have a snack. How are you, boss?' he asks Henry. 'Have you had a nice time with Juno?'

'Yep,' says Henry, looking shifty.

'Thanks for looking after the boys, sweetheart,' Mum says, coming over and sitting down in the armchair behind me. 'I'm glad you had fun together.'

I don't know that we had *that* much fun, but it seems easier just to nod.

Ed goes out of the room. A few minutes later Josh sidles back in, with a biscuit in one hand, and one in his mouth.

'Josh!' Mum says. 'You know you're not meant to be eating biscuits between meals.'

Josh says furiously, through his biscuit, 'Dad SAID I could! He SAID!'

'OK, fine,' says Mum, caving instantly, but Josh is still indignant and marches out of the room. Henry scurries out after him, looking worried.

'These postcards showing the chalet are nice, aren't they?' says Mum as if nothing's happened. 'You should send one to your dad.'

When does positive thinking become total delusion? I'm not going to send one to Dad. Why would I rub his nose in the fact that I'm having a luxury holiday in a five-star chalet that he could never afford?

Picking them up, I see someone's already written on one of them in drunken, wobbly letters. It says,

ElLa, HELP!
Asutria is Turbul. But there is Wify.
Love Josh

'What does Asutria is Turbul mean?' Mum asks, worried.

'I think it means . . . Austria is Terrible? And I think Wify means Wi-Fi.'

I should feel sorry for Josh, but within seconds Mum and I are both laughing. It's so typical of Josh to send a cry for help but also mention the Wi-Fi.

'Should I throw it out?' I ask Mum.

'No, just leave it. He's not going to figure out how to post it.'

I run upstairs, thinking I'd better get a head start on deciding what to wear. I can hear Henry and Josh playing some kind of game with Ed in the kitchen. As I round the bend in the wooden stairs, I look out the window at the sunset, which is purple and green with streaks of yellow, and I suddenly feel completely, ridiculously happy. How did *that* happen?

18

The Buddha Bar, where I'm meeting Tara, does not look very Zen. This is the night off for most of the staff in the resort and the Buddha has capitalised on this with two-euro shots. It's packed with Australians, Austrians, Italians and French as well as English people, all shouting at each other over the Europop. I can't see Tara, or Lara, so I squeeze myself through the crowds hoping to bump into them.

I'm wearing my favourite black-and-white striped ballet top, and my long black skirt. Of course, everyone else is in jeans. At least my make-up came out OK. I attempted a cat eye, but it went wrong as usual – I'm never going to be a billionaire make-up vlogger – so I settled for a smudgy look instead.

Halfway round, I make eye contact with Boy, who is sitting with his gang of blonde hair-flippers. Pretending not to see him, I turn and go the other way, and finally spot Tara, squashed into a corner.

'Hey!' Tara waves me over. She's with Lara and three sporty guys, dressed in various combinations of T-shirts, bobble hats and snowboarding trousers. One of them is so tanned, it's like he's been deep-fried. Tara's looking amazing in a navy-blue bustier: this must be the famous pulling top.

'Juno, this is Mikey and this is *Rob*,' Tara raises her eyebrows at me as she introduces the tanned guy, 'And this is Stevie . . . guys, this is Juno!'

'Hi, babe! Great to see you!' adds Lara, giving me a big hug. She has had a few Jagerbombs, I think. She's wearing a skin-tight red number that shows a massive amount of cleavage. Mikey, in particular, can't stop staring at it.

Lara turns to me. 'What do you want to drink?'

'Oh, I'll get it,' I say quickly, but Lara insists and gets a round of Baileys, Jagerbombs and massive beer steins for the boys. It turns out that Mikey is a chalet host and Stevie is a driver. Mikey is Canadian and Rob, the tanned guy who I think Tara wants me to like, is Australian. I nod and listen while he starts talking about snowboarding. I don't fancy him – he's shorter than me for a start, and the tan is too much – but he seems nice enough.

'So what are you into?' asks Rob.

'Um, how do you mean?'

'I dunno . . . what kind of music do you like?'

This question scares me. It's always a trap. There's no

way I'm telling him the truth which is: Taylor Swift and classical stuff.

'I like sort of nineties indie music. Belle and Sebastian? PJ Harvey? That kind of thing.' This is true, mostly: I've listened to loads of Mum and Dad's old CDs.

'Huh,' says Rob. He's not that impressed. 'You like Jamiroquai?'

I don't really know Jamiroquai. 'They're OK?'

Rob laughs. 'So have you done much travelling?' He starts telling me all about his trip backpacking around the world. Another one! Does anyone ever stay home? But he doesn't seem too bad. And he buys me a second Bailey's – I seem to have drunk my first one quite quickly.

'So did I tell you about Indonesia?' Rob asks, his breath tickling my ear.

'No. Was it good?' I say distractedly. I've just seen Boy, standing at the bar and talking to a woman in her twenties. They're not flirting, just looking as if they're having a really good chat. Rob's story is going on and on, covering several continents, and my mind is wandering just as widely. I'm thinking that even though Boy is moody and full of himself, he's a lot more interesting to talk to. He looks over, and I instantly pretend to be fascinated by Rob's story about getting 'off his face' in Mexico.

'Heyy lovely!' Tara says. 'Come and dance!' And before I can blink, she's dragged me across the room to the microscopic dancefloor.

'Thank you for saving me!' I yell in her ear.

'Didn't you like him?' She dances around me. 'I thought you might, but whatever. Forget those guys, let's have fun!'

It's always embarrassing when you dance with a new friend for the first time. How much eye contact is too much? What if you're acting too sexy and it's creepy? But I love dancing, and soon I let go.

'Oh my God, you're crazy! But in a good way!' yells Tara.

I'm having so much fun. I can't remember the last time I went out. We've all stopped doing it because of the endless grind of study, study, study. But looking around at all the sweaty happy people I think: there is life after A levels.

'Let's get another drink!' I suggest, and run to the bar. I'm so happy that I don't even think about whether the barman will serve me. But miraculously, he does – and even gives me a free shot! I notice in the mirror behind the bar that I'm looking very pink-faced.

'Do I look really sweaty?' I ask Tara, when I get back to her.

'Yes, but everyone's sweaty,' she points out, knocking back her Jagerbomb. 'Don't worry! Drink up!'

Don't worry; drink up. I've had so much advice in my life – advice from Mum, from Emma, from the internet – but there's something I haven't tried.

'It's time for me to let my hair down!' I scream at Tara, undoing my plait and shaking it around.

'Work it, girlfriend!' she yells back, fluffing it up for me. 'Let's dance on the bar!'

Normally I would never agree to something so dangerous, but tonight it seems fine. Tara pulls me up beside her; I nearly fall right off again but then I'm upright and we're dancing! Lara's on the ground taking pictures of us, but I don't know her on any social networks, so it's fine.

'Let's crowd-surf!' Tara shouts. She holds out her hands and jumps forward. Mikey and the other guys catch her, and then they hold out their hands for me.

'Oh, no,' I say, waving my hands in protest. 'Not me. No thanks.' There are limits. I could break my ankle doing that.

'Come on!' Tara yells. 'Just do it, babe!' And their whole group starts chanting 'Ju-no! Ju-no! Ju-no!' Except Mikey, who I think is chanting 'Judo!'

I can't believe I am actually doing this, but I hold out my arms, shut my eyes and jump. And they catch me!

'Amaaazing!' shrieks Tara, hugging me and high-fiving me all at once.

I've crowd-surfed! And then we're dancing around in a sort of circle, and after that, things go blurry. I'm not sure of the exact time frame but I remember teaching Tara and Rob the Thriller dance, and then Mikey shows me the tattoo on his leg, and then the boys are on the bar for some kind of auction, and I win Stevie. Everyone's brilliant, even Rob.

'Everyone needs to have fun from time to time!' I scream at Tara.

'Yes!' she shouts, and whirls me around. 'Look, this is the kind of dancing they do at a Scottish ceilidh! Have you ever been to one?' Without waiting for an answer, she whirls me round like a spinning top, and I'm having the time of my life until I realise that I have about twenty seconds before I throw up. Tearing myself away, I race as fast as I can to the toilet, and charge into a cubicle.

19

When I look in the mirror my heart almost stops. My mascara has smudged everywhere, I have dark circles under my eyes and my face is even more red than usual. I look like a clown who's been in a bar fight. What is Mum going to say when she sees me? What is Mum going to say when she *smells* me?

Tara charges into the bathroom, holding a glass of water. 'There you are! That's good. Better out than in,' she says, handing it to me. 'Sip that, don't swig it or it'll all come up again.'

'I don't feel so fantastic. Maybe I should go and lie in the snow or something,' I say, while repairing the smears under my eyes with Vaseline.

Tara hands me some mints. 'We're all going somewhere with Mikey,' she says. 'He's got the key to a place with a Jacuzzi – it's meant to be awesome.'

That sounds a bit much. My mouth's too full of mints to say no, but I shake my head.

'You had a bit of an audience during your dance, by the way,' Tara stage-whispers, as we head back into the bar.

I clasp my hand over my mouth. 'My mum?' I whisper.

'Yes, Juno, your mum was watching the whole thing and cheering along. No, your hairy neighbour.' Tara raises her eyebrows and makes a subtle head movement behind her where Boy is leaning against the bar. He's all alone.

'Let's go over and say hi,' says Tara.

'Oh, no, Tara, don't.'

But it's too late. She's dragged me over to the bar, where she asks me, 'Now what would you like, darling? Oh, hello,' she adds, looking up at Boy. 'Had a good night?'

'Not bad,' he says. 'Do you two want a drink?'

'Heyyy,' says a voice behind us. It's one of the 'chalet princesses'. She's the blondest and flickiest of all of them, with heavy eyeliner.

'Hi, Millie,' says Tara. 'How are you?'

'I'm okaaay,' she says, in a moaning voice. 'Except for wasting my night off here.' She scrunches up her nose. 'I hate it . . . it's sooo full of chavs.' She glances at me.

'Well, there's one less now!' I say brightly. 'I'm going home. Bye!' I grab Tara and we run out of the bar together, giggling.

Outside, Tara tells the others what happened and I receive multiple high-fives as we stumble down the street. We've lost Rob, but we've gained someone else called Dippy who is somehow connected with the Jacuzzi place.

'Did she say she wishes she was in Verbier? That's all I've ever heard her say,' says Lara.

'I didn't think you had it in you,' says Mikey. Which doesn't seem like a compliment but I know what he means.

'Come for a nightcap to celebrate,' says Tara.

'Definitely not. I'm meant to be home by now.' I fend off their offers to walk me back. 'It's literally three minutes away and there are loads of people around. Go, have fun.'

I'm smiling to myself as I walk along our street. What a great night. The air is so fresh, and it's quiet – if you ignore the techno pounding from the stone-clad bars. I can also see stars: millions of them. I crane my head, trying to look at them all, and end up going round in a circle or two before I arrive at our chalet.

I reach into the space under the shoe-rack on the porch, where the key will be waiting for me. Except it's not.

'OK,' I say to myself. 'Do not panic. It will be somewhere.'

Using the torch on my phone, I do a forensic-style shake-down of the whole porch. Nothing. I dial Mum's number, but her phone is switched off. Ed's goes straight to voicemail too. I have a brief panic that they've both been abducted and murdered – but then I remember there's no reception in their bedroom. There isn't even a doorbell to the chalet. I stare at my phone, hoping it will come up with some kind of solution.

Finally, I take my remaining coins and fling them at Mum and Ed's bedroom window. But they miss by miles, and now, as well as being locked out, I'm down eighty cents.

'You want to bring your shoulder further back,' says a voice behind me. 'And loosen your wrist.'

Before I even turn around I know that it's Boy. I am not in the mood.

'Yeah, that's . . . Thanks.' I turn back and get ready to throw my last coin – a euro.

'Stop!' He leaps forward and grabs my hand. 'That's a lot of money to some people. Try some cents instead.'

Taking some coins from his pocket, he flings them at the window. They hit it with a satisfying few clicks, before falling deep in the snow.

'You'll have to let me know how much I owe you,' I say, hoping my sarcastic tone will cover the wobble in my voice.

'It's fine,' he says. 'I don't have any more change, though. Have you tried just yelling?'

I shake my head, silently. There are some things I'm just not prepared to do, and yelling 'Mum' in the street in the middle of the night is one of them.

'Why don't you call Tara? She'll have a key.'

'Good idea,' I mutter. I can't believe I didn't think of it before. I can get the key off Tara without having to join them all in the Jacuzzi. But there's no reply.

With perfect timing, little white flakes have started to float down in a chilly multitude from the sky.

'Looks like you'll be sleeping in the Athena,' says Boy.

'As if! That's a five-star hotel!'

'Surely you could put it on your dad's credit card?'

'For the last time, he is not my dad. He's my stepfather. And if you think a euro isn't a lot of money to me, you're nuts. Didn't your friend just call me a chav?'

'She didn't—' He breaks off. 'I'm sorry,' he says eventually. 'I shouldn't have said that about your dad's credit card. Stepdad's.'

'Or his Mercedes.'

'His Mercedes?' He looks at me blankly, then laughs. 'Oh. I forgot about that. But you *had* just accused me of melting all the snow off Everest and ruining the planet with my selfish trips.'

'That's not what I said!'

'Look; forget all that. What are you going to do now? Because you can't sit out here all night. It's dangerous.'

I look at him sceptically. 'I thought you were a fan of danger.'

'I like the right kind. But it seems a bit pointless to get hypothermia sitting in the middle of a ski resort.'

Hypothermia! I definitely don't want to get hypothermia.

After a pause, he says, 'You could come and wait at my place. Just until someone calls you back.'

Wait at his place? I'm sure he doesn't want me to do that and anyway, wouldn't it be really awkward?

'No, it's OK, I can wait here. On the porch. It's not *too* cold . . . And I've got a coat.'

'Yeah, sure,' he says. 'Who needs ten fingers anyway, right?'

Me! I need ten fingers. Especially in A level year.

'OK,' I say reluctantly. 'Let's go.'

20

Tara was right. Boy's place *is* above a garage, an old-fashioned one round the corner from our place. Boy opens a metal door, whips out a torch, and the light reveals concrete walls and an iron staircase.

'It's up here . . . Mind the gaps, it's a bit rusty.'

It certainly is: there are a few steps missing, and I'm clinging to the rail in terror as I inch after him. When we get to the top, there's another concrete corridor, with a bulb hanging from a wire. It's a health-and-safety nightmare.

Opening a further door, he leads me into a big, bare room, lit by another bare light bulb. Maybe 'room' is pushing it; it's more like a garage or a loft. There's a kitchen corner, a sagging blue sofa, a single bed and a tall cubicle thing with a curtain in the middle of the room. I have a horrible feeling that's his shower.

'It's nice!' I say, looking around. 'It's . . . big.'

He laughs, and I realise he's embarrassed. 'I don't normally have visitors. Are you cold? Take that.' He shrugs off his parka and hands it to me, before plugging in a standing heater.

'I'll put on some tea and it'll warm up in a bit,' he says. 'It's not fancy but it's cheap – almost free in fact.'

'Sure. No, it's cool. It's . . . different.' I slip on his parka, which is still warm from his body.

Boy is at the hob, heating some water in a saucepan. He smiles properly for the first time since we got here. 'It's *different*,' he says, imitating me. 'Really? Or are you being polite?'

My answer comes out without me being able to stop it. 'It's a *bit* like the den of a serial killer.'

For a second I think I've offended him, but then he starts laughing. He looks completely different when he laughs: much younger, and nicer.

'Hey, don't hold back. Tell me what you really think.'

'I don't mean that you're actually a serial killer,' I protest.

'How do I know *you're* not a serial killer? That whole thing with the key could have been a ruse.'

'That's true.'

I relax, deciding that a serial killer probably wouldn't make me tea or give me his parka to wear before murdering me. Looking around, I notice lots of contraptions scattered everywhere: pieces of wood and tin cans with wires, and something that looks like a table bolted onto a skateboard. There's also a giant map of the world taped up with Blu-Tack, with a red circle somewhere north of India. The Himalayas, I presume.

'I'm sorry I said that about you destroying Everest,' I say. 'It wasn't fair. You're right. I'm not exactly living off the grid myself.'

'It's OK. It was a good point.' He hands me a mug of tea. 'Hang on, I'll just pull down the milk . . .'

Hopping up on a chair, he tugs at a pulley contraption that connects to a small window. It opens, letting a flood of icy air in, and the pulley descends with a carton of milk on it, as well as cheese and ham.

'What *is* that?'

'It's my fridge pulley,' he says, like it's the most normal thing in the world. He hands me the milk and then cranks the pulley up and out the window again.

I'm actually rather impressed. He might be eccentric but he's certainly independent – compared to me, anyway.

Suddenly there's a mewing sound; a black cat with one white paw has padded forward to meet us.

'Oh, she's so sweet! Is she yours?' I hold out a hand to her but she ignores me.

'No. She just visits sometimes.' He strokes her. 'Generally whenever she senses milk or food. Her name's Meribel.' He hands me the warm, furry bundle.

'She's adorable!' I'm hoping Meribel will stay with me, but she slips out of my hands and runs to curl up in Boy's lap instead.

We sip our tea in silence for a minute while I wonder what to say next.

'So do you always dance on bars like that?' he asks.

'Oh! No. Tara must have talked me into it.'

'I heard about you helping her out,' he says. 'Tara, I mean. That was pretty cool of you. I think that's the first time I've heard of a guest doing something like that.'

I won't lie: I don't hate that he's described me as 'pretty cool'.

'It was kind of fun in a way. Anyway . . .' I look at the table to avoid his gaze. 'Um . . . nice Christmas card!' I say randomly.

'Oh yeah. It's from my brothers.' He picks it up. 'I was over here for Christmas so they sent me that and a bottle of brandy.'

'You were here at *Christmas*?' This shocks me because Christmas is totally sacred to me – from opening presents together to eating our traditional Crispy Prawn Won Tons in front of the TV. They've been discontinued now – like our family Christmas itself. 'What did you do?'

'I went to my landlord's house and we had an eight-course dinner with champagne, pudding, the works. And then there was a party for some of the Aussies and Kiwis who stayed as well.'

I'm about to ask him more – such as whether his parents minded – but I'm distracted by the sight of his big, brown hand moving over the cat's head.

'So how old are you?' I ask instead.

'Nine hundred and ninety-two,' he says, promptly. 'I'm an immortal vampire.'

'Sure.'

'OK. I'm nineteen. How old are you?'

'Seventeen.'

Just then there's a muffled sound from my pocket. I reach for my phone instantly, thinking it must be Mum, but it's Jack. *Can't sleep. Keep thinking maybe I should go into Starbucks tomorrow and have one more try. What do you think?* But I can't concentrate on Jack's love life right now.

'Sorry, I thought that might be my mum,' I mutter.

'Do you want to try ringing her again?'

I don't, but I call her anyway and get her voicemail. I send a text and hope she doesn't see it for a while.

'So . . . do you not normally hang out with Tara?' I ask, in an effort to continue normal conversation.

'Not really. I mainly hang out with the other guys who were at my instructor school, at the Arlberg. And some of them know Millie and her friends from school.' He shrugs.

'Sure. And . . . sorry, did you say Millie was your girlfriend?' I say, trying to sound casual.

'Nope,' he says, inspecting the sole of his trainer. 'I don't have a girlfriend.'

I don't have a girlfriend. The five most thrilling words in the English language – depending on who says them. For some reason, I shiver.

'Are you still cold?' he says. 'Here – have this.'

He produces a blanket, and is about to chuck it when he changes his mind and puts it round me instead. Which means that his arms are on me, briefly. It's only a few seconds. But those few seconds are about a million times more exciting than anything I ever had with Jack.

He doesn't move away. His knee is curled up on the sofa, touching the side of my body, and his elbow is touching mine. And though we start talking about other things I'm only half able to concentrate, because I'm so busy feeling him leaning against me, and wondering if he can feel it, too.

'It's a pity I don't have a fire,' he's saying. 'I was tempted to get an old oil can and burn fuel in it, but the lack of chimney is a problem. Don't want to die of smoke inhalation.'

'Actually,' I say without thinking. 'That's my plan, if ever I'm burned at the stake. I would inhale really deeply, and then there's a good chance I'd die of smoke inhalation before the flames started to burn.'

'You have a plan . . . for if you're ever burned at the stake?' We both start laughing. 'That's pretty dark,' he says.

'By the way – what is *this*?' I reach out with my toes to touch his skateboard table.

'Oh. I thought it would be handy to have a table that moved about.'

'How did you learn to do all that?'

Boy starts telling me about growing up in the middle

of nowhere, and escaping into the shed and having the time of his life sawing things and taking things apart and hammering nails into his fingers. At some point I realise I'm exhausted, so I close my eyes to listen better, until I float into the darkness on the sound of his voice.

21

I'm woken by something soft and furry tapping at me. It's Meribel. She looks at me indignantly before going over to Boy, and standing on his face, miaowing. He swats her away, while I sit up, dazed. I'm in Boy's place, and I fell asleep. How embarrassing.

I'm relieved that he seems just as discombobulated as me.

'I wasn't asleep,' he says. 'I was dozing. OK, Meribel. Don't eat me.' He gets up, still in his clothes from last night, and rummages for cat food and a tin opener. Meribel's so frantic she keeps getting in his way as he puts out her food and water.

'I was asleep,' I admit, yawning. The windows in the top of the room have turned from black to grey. I grab my phone, and almost faint with relief when I see there's nothing from Mum.

'I should go.' I stand up.

'OK . . . I'll walk you,' he says, scratching at his beard. 'Urgh. I wish I could shave.'

'Why can't you?'

'Because my tan only goes halfway down my face – and I don't want to scare the kids. I only grew it to make them respect me.'

This makes me laugh. I'm really thirsty now, so I drink water from a glass that I think was stolen from the Foxy Fox, and then shyly ask Boy where his bathroom is. It's down the corridor and even more freezing cold, but at least he has one. I thought he might use a bucket or something. I'm afraid of what I might see in the cracked mirror, but I look more or less OK.

As we go down his rusty stairs, I'm stunned at everything that's happened. This time yesterday I barely knew Boy and now I don't want to say goodbye.

It's freezing outside and incredibly still apart from one bird singing in the distance. There's nobody around except us. I allow myself a brief daydream that there *has* been a nuclear disaster and there's no one left in the world but me and Boy. Not that I want all my friends and family to perish, but if they did, this would be a compensation.

'Let's take a quick detour,' he says. 'I want to show you something.'

'OK.'

We turn up a wooded hill. As we walk the sky grows lighter and a pink streak builds on the horizon. We round another corner, and find ourselves in a small clearing.

We're standing in a world of white and pink: white fields and trees and snowy rooftops, with a rosy wash over it all. As we watch, the shadow gradually recedes and the rosy-pink intensifies, until the whole landscape is bathed in pink and gold, under a pale blue sky. It's the most beautiful thing I've ever seen.

Neither of us says anything. We just stand in silence, breathing it all in.

And then he takes my hand.

He doesn't look at me, but he continues to hold my hand as we walk back to the village. I half-expect him to drop it as soon as we see people. But he keeps holding it, all the way back to my place, where one of the curtains has opened. Mum or Ed must be awake.

My heart is going fast, and everything is so quiet, I'm sure he can hear it. We're nearly at my place, just a few more feet. It's going to happen. We're going to kiss.

I turn to him.

'Well – bye,' I say, barely able to meet his eye. 'Thanks for taking me in.'

'Bye,' he says softly. 'I'll see you soon, yeah?'

I'm looking up, wondering if this is going to be *it*, when there's a hideous grinding noise, and one of the green snow-sweeping carts goes right by us. The driver gives us a wave. '*Guten tag.*'

'*Guten tag.*' Boy drops my hand and we both wave back.

I'm so embarrassed. This whole thing is going to become a farce unless I put a stop to it right now. So I say goodbye for a second time and run up the steps of the chalet. I've just raised my hand to knock on the door, when I feel a tap on my shoulder.

'Wait a second,' he says. And then he kisses me.

The whole world falls away and there's nothing except this kiss. His hands are cold on my face, and I can hear his heart beating, even louder than mine. I don't know how long it lasts, but for however long it is, I'm in heaven.

'I'd better go,' he says, smiling. I nod, then pull him back to kiss him one more time.

And that's when the door opens and we jump apart.

'*Juno*?' says Mum.

22

I want to die. I wish this was a film or a game so I could rewind, pause, erase – basically do anything but stand here looking at Boy's face, and Mum's.

'What the – it's six thirty a.m.! Where have you *been*?' I've never seen her so angry. 'And who are *you*?' she adds.

'Mum, stop! I was locked out, OK? You didn't leave the key. So I had to go to Boy's.'

'What boys?'

'Boy's place! This is Boy! My instructor, remember?' Somehow I thought that would help but Mum just becomes even more freaked out. She clutches her dressing gown around her – a silky, sexy number that she bought when we moved in with Ed. Why can't she wear towelling dressing gowns like normal mothers?

'Your instructor?' She turns to Boy. 'How *old* are you?'

I'm about to say he's only nineteen, when he says angrily, 'It was minus five and she was locked out.'

I don't think this is going to help. 'You should just go home,' I tell him quietly.

'Fine,' he says, and walks off, while Mum glares after him.

A minute ago I was walking on air and now I'm in hell. I'm so humiliated, furious at Mum for being rude to Boy, and mortified that he had to see that. How can it be such a drama that I've been out all night? Particularly since it's not even my fault!

I try to storm past Mum to my room, but she grabs me.

'No you don't! We need to discuss this.' She makes me sit down on the sofa with her. 'Tell me what happened.'

'Mum! Stop! Literally nothing happened. We went back to his place and we had tea. And I played with his cat. And then we fell asleep.'

She looks confused. 'Is that a euphemism or something? "I played with his cat"?'

'No! Oh my God. He has an actual cat. And then we both fell asleep.'

'Are you *sure* that was all?'

That's enough. She's already ruined our first kiss. I'm not going to let her ruin every single memory of last night. I stand up.

'Mum, I'm not discussing this with you anymore. Either you believe me or you don't.' And I run upstairs, closing the door behind me and curling up under my duvet. I wriggle out of my clothes, and something falls out of my coat pocket. It's the taxi card Boy gave me. I clutch it in my hand and close my eyes. Not even the smell of bacon frying downstairs can keep me awake.

23

Slowly opening my eyes, I see that it's around four. It takes me a few minutes to figure out that it's p.m., not a.m. Totally disoriented, I lie there wondering what's going on – and then I remember. Boy. The whole night seems like a dream. But it's soon shattered by a loud knock on the door.

'Come in,' I mutter.

'It's four o'clock, Juno,' Mum says, poking her head round the door. 'We're having tea in twenty minutes. You slept the whole day.'

'I know,' I yawn.

'Look. I overreacted earlier.' She leans forward. 'Of course I believe you, Ju. I'm sorry. It's just that things are so different now from when I was young.'

This is one of Mum's favourite topics; you would think she was a hundred the way she goes on about it. Things that didn't exist when she was my age include:

nut allergies, Facebook, Netflix and Al-Qaida. Also, she didn't see a squirrel until she moved to London when she was twenty-three.

'It seems so unlikely that a boy his age would just – that you'd just talk all night.'

I wish she would stop. It's none of her business if something did happen. And I'm already forgetting what it was like to kiss Boy – and sit on his couch with him, and watch the sunrise together.

'It was only a kiss,' I say, my voice trembling.

Mum looks regretful. 'I know. Look, why don't you give him a call and meet up for a coffee or something? Tell him your silly mum overreacted.'

I roll over. 'Thanks. But after what happened this morning, I'll probably never see him again.'

This seems to annoy her all over again and she stands up. 'Oh, come on, Juno. Your life is not a tragedy!'

And she flounces out. What was that for? I thought it was teenagers who were meant to be drama queens!

I reach for my phone for comfort. An alert flashes. Seventy-two days to A levels. Then I remember to message Jack back, telling him I don't think it *is* a good idea to go back after Starbucks Boy and that I'll talk to him later.

I have a new voice message. I hardly ever get voice messages; whenever I do I feel positive that I'm being arrested or something. I listen cautiously.

'Hey. It's me . . . Hope you haven't got in too much trouble. So if you are allowed out again, do you want to go skiing tomorrow morning? I've got the day off. Gimme a call. Bye.'

He called! He must have got my number from the ski school. I'm so nervous I have to make several attempts before I can dial his number.

'Hello?' It's noisy. He's obviously walking along in the village or something.

'Hi, it's me. Juno.'

'I know. Are you in trouble?'

'No, no. It's OK.'

'Good. So do you want to go skiing tomorrow? I would say meet tonight, but I'm a bit knackered for some reason.' I think I can hear him smiling.

He tells me to meet him at one of the ski lifts on the other side of the village, at ten.

'So – see you then?'

'Sure.'

'OK. Bye.' He clears his throat. 'Look forward to it.'

'Me too.' There's a brief silence, and then I hang up, barely able to believe it. He's asked me out. I'm seeing him tomorrow.

I pull on some clothes, splash cold water on my face, brush my teeth and run downstairs. Everyone is in front of the fire; Tara is pouring tea, and the boys are carrying a tray of cookies, fresh from the oven, watched by Mum. Ed is pacing around and making a work call. 'No, Simon! Forget the blackberries! It's got to be blueberries.' Everything is the same, but everything is different, because I'm seeing Boy tomorrow. I feel a massive wave of affection for them all, especially Mum. I give her a hug, and she hugs me back, looking surprised but pleased.

'Cookie?' Josh asks, holding out a plate.

'Yes, please! These look amazing – did you make them?'

'Me and Henry did,' Josh says. 'Siobhan helped,' he adds, fairly.

'You seem very happy,' Mum says. 'Did you . . .' She's obviously realised that I've heard from Boy. 'Have you – are you planning to meet up again?' she asks, casually.

'He wants to take me skiing tomorrow. I can, can't I?'

Tara looks excited. 'Wait a second . . .' She cocks her head on one side. 'Not . . . the Gruffalo?'

I nod, totally unable to hide my grin.

'Sorry, who are we talking about?' says Ed. 'Have I missed something?'

'Nothing,' Mum says to Ed. 'Just girl talk.'

'Yuk,' says Josh.

24

Everybody looks identical in ski gear – especially when they're all wearing sunglasses or visors. I'm used to seeing Boy in his instructor's uniform, too. So even though I know exactly what he looks like, I still have to double-check so that I don't go up to a complete stranger.

'You ready to hop on?' he asks, pointing at the lift behind us.

'This one?' I ask, panicked. 'I thought we were going on the gondola lift.'

'This is a gondola lift.'

I thought a gondola was like a chair lift. This one is like the carriages on the London Eye, except that it hangs from a single thread and goes miles up into the air.

'It'll take us to a very quiet blue slope,' Boy explains. 'Great views. I think you'll like it.'

I shake my head. 'I'm sorry. I can't get in that lift.'

He looks surprised, and disappointed, but he doesn't say anything except, 'Well . . . OK. We'll do something else. Let me think.'

He glances at his watch, while I look at the people getting on the gondola. Some of them are actual children. About two feet high. If they can do it . . . Surely it can't be that dangerous?

'Fine. I'll do it.'

'Great!' he says, looking pleased.

We get in the queue and minutes later, we're in the lift, soaring miles above the ground. I'm aware of Boy chatting to me, but I can't say anything except the odd 'Mm'. The cables holding us up are so thin; a hand could snap them.

'Are you all right?' Boy says.

I can't reply. My mouth is dry.

'Oh.' He frowns. 'We're nearly there.' He reaches an arm out and presses me close to him. I concentrate on the feel of his ski-suit, and the warmth of his body, and tell myself it's OK.

By the time the lift gets to the end, my legs are shaking so much that I can barely walk out.

'That wasn't so bad, was it?' Boy asks.

I glare at him.

'You look like you're about to hit me,' he says. 'I promise it's worth it. Come on. I want to show you something.'

We ski a little distance until we come to a sort of

viewing platform full of people taking photos. The sun is so dazzling that at first I can't see a thing. Then the landscape comes into focus; a 360-degree panorama of white peaks and dark shadows, silhouetted against the blue sky. We're so high up, I can almost see the curve of the Earth.

'It feels as if we're on top of the world,' I say.

'Yeah. We're not, though. That would be the Himalayas.'

'Oh,' I say, respectfully. But then I decide I don't want to be *too* respectful.

'Well, we can't all go to the *Himalayas*,' I say. 'Or climb Everest.'

He slides away from me, laughing. 'Let's go this way.'

It's strange how quickly I've become at home in this new element. It's like learning to swim: you can't even remember what it was like before. The snow's smooth, the slope is gentle, the air is fresh and sparkling. It's heaven.

'I can finally see what all the fuss is about,' I call over to Boy, who grins and gives me a thumbs-up.

We spend another hour or so skiing, before we arrive at a little café in the mountains, with a panoramic terrace and people sitting outside wearing sunglasses. We sit on the terrace and order *Schinken-Käse* – ham and cheese sandwiches – and hot chocolate. He orders in German, which I find impressive.

'I can't believe you know the German for marshmallows.'

'*Mäusespeck*. It's about the only German I do know,' he says. 'I think it means Mouse Ham. That's what I like to picture anyway – a little mouse holding a big piece of ham.' He starts laughing like a lunatic.

'Very mature,' I say, laughing. It's the kind of thing that Emma would find funny, too. I end up telling him all about Emma and how she has a really silly sense of humour – but still worries about her school work all the time.

'She shouldn't,' he says, shaking his head. 'I mean seriously, what's the point? It all seems so important when you're in school, but when you step outside into the real world . . .' He gestures at the sunny scene around us. 'It's just not. Important, I mean.'

I nod, thinking that if I didn't like him so much, it could get annoying the way he keeps on telling me how much better the 'real world' is than school.

'Hey,' I say, playfully. 'Just out of interest. Is Boy . . .'

He laughs. 'My real name? Nope. It's a nickname.'

'So what is your real name?'

'I'm afraid that's classified,' he says. 'But I can reveal that . . . Let's see. My dad is a teacher – he teaches economics. My mum died when I was nine. And I've got two older brothers, Theo and Hugh.'

I feel so awful about his mum that I switch to a more neutral subject. 'What are your brothers like?'

'They're cool. Hugh is a doctor. He's the clever one. And Theo runs his own IT business. Come to think of it, he's the clever one as well. I'm the thick one.'

'You're not thick!' I protest.

He shrugs. 'I failed my A levels. Geography and physics, anyway. I got a B in maths.'

'But maths is one of the hardest subjects! Did you have a bad teacher or something?'

'I'm dyslexic.'

'Oh!' I'm surprised he's made such a big thing of it. 'But that's nothing! Tons of people I know have dyslexia. Didn't you have special help in school?'

'Yes, but it took them ages to diagnose me. The initial diagnosis was that I was a little brat. Which was also true.' He grins. 'Anyway . . . it wasn't a big deal. I haven't done too badly.'

'No, of course not! But if you did want to re-apply for uni – you could easily get more help, even now . . .'

'I could, but I don't want to. I'm doing fine.' He stands up, without looking at me. 'You ready?'

He leads the way out of the restaurant and we click our skis back on in silence. I'm wondering if I've offended him somehow, when he turns to me. 'By the way. You've managed to stop me littering. See?' And he tucks his cigarette stub into the pocket of his ski jacket. 'I don't drop them on the ground anymore. In fact . . .' He pulls out a small handful. 'I need to do a clear-out.'

'That's revolting,' I laugh. I don't want to admit that it's also possibly the most romantic thing anyone's ever done for me.

25

We spend the rest of the afternoon skiing, until the shadows start lengthening over the snow.

'Give me those,' Boy says, as we wander back towards the village. And, taking my skis, he puts them over his shoulder. Which is even more romantic than the cigarette stubs.

'They don't seem to have many Easter eggs here, do they?' I say, as we pass a few shop windows.

'No. They obviously agree with my dad.'

'How so?'

'He's not into Easter eggs, so we never had them. I remember one Easter, when I was about eleven, I bought myself one with my pocket money. He told me that was really stupid because I could have got much more chocolate for the same amount of money if I'd just bought bars.'

He seems to find this funny but I think it's awful. What a Grinch.

'But it's not the amount of chocolate! It's the joy of the egg . . .'

'For my dad, the real joy is pointing out when I've done something stupid.' Boy grins at me. 'Anyway, I prefer Kinder eggs now. I like making the toy.'

I'm about to ask him more when I notice a tall blonde figure approaching. It's Millie.

'Hiiiiii,' she says, stopping beside us. 'What's going on here?'

Boy says, 'Just hanging out. You?'

'Does Tabitha know about this?' Millie asks, lowering her voice as if she's talking about a national-security issue.

'Mind your own business,' Boy says. 'Come on, Juno.'

We walk in silence for a minute before I ask, 'Who's Tabitha?'

'She's my ex . . . but it's been over for a while. Millie's her friend, and she's nuts. She's always stirring.'

I nod, but I feel like I've been punched in the stomach. I'd be crazy to think he'd never had a girlfriend, but the thought of someone else with him, in his place, on that sofa . . . I can't bear to think about it. When my phone rings, I grab it, happy to have a distraction.

'Juno,' says Mum, 'I was thinking. Why don't you ask your friend if he'd like to come for dinner?'

I look sideways at Boy, wondering if he can hear.

'Mum, really?' Has she forgotten what their last meeting was like? 'He's probably busy.'

'Well, ask him, won't you? We'll be nice, I promise.'

After I've hung up, Boy asks, 'What am I too busy for?'

'Mum wants me to invite you for dinner. But you don't have to come – I mean, you probably don't want to deal with all that.'

'Course not,' Boy says. 'I'd much rather open a tin in my room and have dinner with Meribel. I'm being sarcastic, by the way.'

'Are you sure?' I ask, amazed.

'Yeah, I'm sure. Unless you don't want me to?'

'No, I do. I'd love you to.' As we turn towards my place, I add, 'Just promise me you won't believe anything my mum says, OK?'

26

Mum opens the door before I've even knocked. She must have been hovering inside.

'Hello!' She smiles warmly at Boy. 'I'm Siobhan. It's nice to meet you. I am sorry if I was a little ... edgy yesterday.'

Boy looks wary, but shakes her hand politely.

'How tall are you?' asks Josh.

'Six foot three.'

'Why are you called Boy? Don't you have a real name?' asks Henry. Boy laughs.

'Boys! Don't be rude!' says Ed. He comes over to shake Boy's hand. 'Good to meet you. Henry, do you want to help Tara set the table?'

'No thank you,' says Henry, sliding away.

Tara grabs a beer out of the fridge for Boy, and gives me an excited 'Whattttt?' look. I smile awkwardly. We're all eating together tonight –

including the boys – which I hope will provide some distraction.

'So do you snowboard as well as ski?' Mum asks, trying to 'draw him out'. She's normally quite good at doing this with new people, but it doesn't seem to be working with Boy.

'No, I just ski.'

'Any particular reason?' she asks.

'Not really – I just prefer it.'

Mum smiles politely, but I can tell she's disappointed he's not more chatty. It was so different when Jack came to dinner. He raved about Mum's lamb shanks, and he and Mum bonded over some old film called *Moonstruck*. Boy is never going to rave about lamb shanks – or about Tara's delicious roast beef. But I wish he would show his personality a bit more, the way he does when he's with me.

'Did you know Boy is planning on climbing Everest in the summer?' I say.

'Everest! Nice! Good for you,' says Ed.

'Isn't Everest very dangerous?' says Mum.

'Sure . . . But it's good to take a few risks.'

Mum looks horrified; I feel like burying my face in my hands. Whatever you want the boy you like to say to your mum, 'it's good to take a few risks' isn't it.

Ed asks Boy, 'Speaking of, um, mountains . . . are there any wolves in Austria?'

Wolves? I think Ed did mean to help me out, but did he have to pick that topic? I'm now picturing a wolf pack roaming the baby slopes and picking off the worst skiers.

'No, I don't think so,' Boy says. 'I doubt the farmers here would allow it. I tell you what I have seen though: hedgehogs.'

'Really?' I ask, enchanted. 'Aren't they hibernating?'

'You would think so, but actually they tend to change nests once or twice a winter, so you occasionally see them.' He goes on for a while about hedgehogs and their habits, and concludes, 'They're shy, but they have a lot of personality.' He smiles at me, as if he's been reading my mind.

'I'm finished. Can I have some brownies?' asks Josh.

'What's the magic word?' says Ed.

'Wingardium leviosa!' says Josh. I notice Mum open her mouth to say something, but then she smiles instead. Josh adds, 'Pleeeease.'

'I can do turning already in skiing,' Henry confides to Boy.

Ed and Josh help Tara dish out ice-cream and brownies, as we all discuss parallel turns versus snowplough turns. I would have found this so boring a week ago, but now we're all equally obsessed. And it's lovely to see Boy starting to relax and be himself – chatting about the resort staff and gossip.

'By the way,' says Tara. 'You know SJ, who ate the bad oyster? She's quit.'

'It's a bit late for the mid-season blues, isn't it?' says Boy.

'What does that mean?' Mum asks.

'It normally happens around February – when people fall out with their boss, or break up with someone, and they drop out,' he says.

'Which was it with SJ?' asks Ed, looking amused.

'Nobody knows. It was rucksacks at dawn,' Tara says.

Josh looks bored. 'Do you want to play Top Trumps with us?' he asks Boy. 'It's superheroes.'

'Oh, you don't have to—' I'm sure that's the last thing he wants to do. But Boy nods.

'Sure. Can Juno play too?'

The game is a lot of fun. There are a couple of times where I have to subtly prompt Boy, when he's slow to read the characters' names and attributes. The boys don't notice though; they're too busy desperately trying to hang on to the Hulk and Spiderman. Boy doesn't let them win, the way I do. He's competitive, but they love it. I feel as bereft as them when eventually he says he has to leave.

'Thanks for dinner. It was really good.' He smiles at Ed and Mum, and they beam back. I think it was playing cards with the boys that finally got him his gold star.

'It was lovely to meet you,' says Mum.

'Come back any time,' says Josh graciously.

Outside, I begin, 'I'm sorry that was so—' but I'm interrupted by him kissing me.

'That was so what?' he murmurs a minute later.

'Embarrassing,' I manage to say.

'No, it was nice. They're cool, your family. They're very relaxed.'

'Really?' He obviously has a very different definition of 'relaxed' from me. But I'm glad he had a good time.

'So do you want to go skiing tomorrow afternoon? I've got lessons till two, but I'm free after that.'

'I'd love to.'

He's kissed me again, and stepped off the porch, before I remember: Mum made a point of wanting us to go skiing together, 'as a family'. For our last afternoon. And I don't think she'll be at all relaxed about me missing it.

27

'So,' Boy says, as we queue for the lift, 'I thought today, you could try your first red slope?'

Miracles do happen. Mum was totally cool about me bailing on our family afternoon and going skiing with Boy instead. And she seems to like him, too. She said he was 'interesting' – which isn't always a compliment, but in this case she swore it was.

'I know he's not as chatty as Jack,' I said, thinking of how well Mum got on with him.

'Well, that's not everything,' said Mum. 'Jack is a lovely boy and I hope you stay friends – but let's face it, he was never shopping in your aisle.'

The only cloud on the horizon is the fact that I'm leaving tomorrow. And the fact that Boy wants us to do some riskier skiing today.

'I'm not sure. I know I've come on a lot, but . . .'

He looks disappointed, then he says, 'OK. We can do another route.'

Now I feel pathetic. I've come on so much; why am I still scared?

'Why so sad?' he asks. 'Anyone would think it wasn't a perfect skiing day.' The chair lift arrives and I have a minute to think over my reply as we buckle ourselves in side by side.

'Nothing,' I say, as we start to crank up into the air. 'Just sorry to cramp your style.'

'Hold these,' he says, handing me his ski poles. I do, and he wriggles his arm out from under the bar and puts it around me.

'Listen,' he says. 'It's really fine. As long as you don't throw up on me then as far as I'm concerned, you're the perfect ski companion.'

I start to laugh. 'Did one of your pupils really throw up on you?'

'Oh yeah. Well, not on me but on my skis.' He rotates his skis, examining them. 'I think I got it all off, but still.'

'Ugh.' I wrinkle my nose in sympathy.

'They're kids. These things happen.' He rubs his nose and frowns. 'But about the red slope – I can go down a red, or a black, or go off-piste any time I want, after you've gone. But I won't be able to hang out with you. So.'

I look at him, his profile tanned against the white mountain, and I know that I'll remember this moment for ever.

'Time for take-off,' Boy says, as we approach the end of the lift. 'You ready? Three, two, one, lift the barrier . . . Now jump.'

We ski off, and come to a pause at the top of a broad, meandering slope, with only a few people dotted here and there skiing down in lazy arcs towards a line of fir trees. We join them at a leisurely pace.

'This is fantastic!'

'It's nice, huh?' Boy smiles. 'I don't know why more people don't come here. Woah! Watch out!' He reaches out as a neon blur skids by, almost knocking me off my feet.

Grabbing me to steady me, he says, 'Flipping snowboarders! Are you OK?'

He's still holding me. My face is tilted up to his. It's hard to concentrate on a reply but I manage, 'Yeah. I'm OK.'

He's staring at me. 'I—'

'You what?' I whisper.

'Nothing. Watch out for those nutters.' He releases me. Leaving me wondering what he was going to say.

'So do you think you'll come back here next year?' I ask eventually.

'Maybe. It depends.'

'On what?'

'On whether something more interesting comes up. I might decide to stay in India and do some more climbing . . . or go diving . . .'

I notice that 'or visit you in London' isn't on his list

of options, but I try not to freak out. After all, what did I really think would happen? I'm going home to do my A levels. He's off to the Himalayas. It's not as though we can meet up in the middle.

'I might come back here though,' he adds, glancing at me. 'It's pretty hard to beat this, isn't it?'

I nod. The cold air, the sunshine, the blue sky. I wish I could bottle it, and take a sniff when I'm back at home, staring at my laptop and slogging through French revision.

'Do you think you'll come back?' he asks. 'Zombie apocalypse permitting?'

'Here, or skiing in general?'

'Either.'

'Well, maybe.' I'm just wondering whether to ask him straight out about us meeting again, when I'm distracted by something ahead.

'Oh,' I say, coming to a halt. This part of the slope suddenly looks much, much steeper. And icy.

'What's wrong?' he asks. 'It's fine. It's still a blue – it's a tad steeper, but it's only this stretch, until the bend.'

I hang back. 'I know, but . . .'

'Come on. You can do this.'

'Could we cut the corner? Over there, by the trees?' I point to a wedge-shaped wooded bit with a field in the middle. 'It looks much flatter.'

'You want to go off-piste?' Boy looks amused. 'We could. Are you sure you'd prefer it?'

'I think so . . . it just looks gentler, doesn't it?'

'Yes, but I don't want you crashing through a random field. I'll go first and see what it's like. Check the snow's not too deep.'

'OK.'

Relieved, I watch him speed off. He's so graceful, skimming along, gathering speed as he zips in and out of the trees and flies across the field of snow. It looks lovely, effortless. I'm tempted to film him but I know my phone won't capture it. I'll remember it instead.

That's when he falls.

28

My first reaction is to laugh. I thought falling over was something that only happened to klutzy beginners like me.

'Bummer!' I yell. 'Are you OK?'

He doesn't reply. And he doesn't move, either. I ski a bit closer and see that he's lying flat on the ground, half-submerged in the snow. One of his skis is sticking straight up in the air, in a way that looks really wrong.

'Juno!' he calls faintly. I start to ski forward but he calls, 'Wait! Stay there!'

Attracted by the shouting, a couple of young English guys wearing novelty frog costumes are heading towards him.

'WAIT!' I yell. 'DON'T MOVE HIM!'

And without thinking, I start forward.

'DON'T TOUCH HIS LEG!' I scream.

They turn round, surprised. As I take in the scene

– Boy sprawled on the ground, his leg twisted at a sickening angle – I feel positive I'm going to throw up.

'Help me get his ski off,' I tell them. 'But please, don't move his leg. Hold it in place.'

Boy doesn't speak – he just lies quietly. He seems calm, but he's breathing quickly and his face is a strange colour.

'Is it really sore?' I ask him.

'No. But you should call the ski patrol. The number's in my—' he winces. 'It's in my phone. But I think I'm lying on it.'

'I've got it!' says one of the frog men. 'I'll call them.'

'Tell them I'm in the wooded bit, just before the turn—' He gives a load of incomprehensible directions. I'm amazed he's so calm.

'They'll be here soon,' one of the frog men says. The other is pouring out a load of irritating chatter. 'Does it hurt? It looks bad. I bet you're in shock. Bad luck! Perfect skiing day. You been out long? How did you end up here?'

'It's fine,' I tell Boy. 'Don't look at it. Just lie there. We're getting help.'

I take off my jacket and put it over him. I've never been so glad in my life that I was paranoid enough to take first-aid lessons. We haven't moved him; he's breathing; we're keeping him warm. Now we just have to wait.

I don't know how long it takes – it could be five minutes, or half an hour – but finally two paramedics arrive on skis. They check Boy's head and leg and ask him a few questions.

'So this is good,' the man says to him, while the woman talks on a walkie-talkie. 'You have no compound fracture, no head injury. We're going to get a sling, and ski you off the mountain. Think you can do that?'

'Yeah,' he says, faintly.

Soon more skiers arrive, carrying a big plastic stretcher, like a hammock. They lift him onto it, and then one of the paramedics asks us to ski with them to the snow-mobile.

I'm not sure that I can keep up, but I don't have much choice. So we set off, all three of us behind Boy. He doesn't move, except occasionally when they go over a bump and he winces. It feels like an eternity before we reach the bottom of the slope.

'Are you OK if we leave you now?' asks a voice. 'Just, we're going to miss our bus back.'

'No – of course. Sure,' I say, dazed. I had forgotten the frog men were even here.

I turn round and see the paramedics strapping Boy's sling to the back of the snow-mobile. One of them explains that they're going to tow him down another slope, to get him to the medical centre.

'Won't that be really painful?' I ask.

'Yeah, it will be tough, but there's no other way. You should ski with us. Give him some encouragement.'

If things were calmer I would explain that I'm not a

very good skier, but within minutes we're all starting off. Boy is bouncing in the sling, with a bit of tarpaulin over his head to shield him from the fumes. We're on harder snow now, and I can see him getting jolted horribly.

'We're nearly there,' I call encouragingly. 'I can see the centre from here.'

He nods and even smiles, though he still looks very glassy-eyed. He must be in unbearable pain. I wish he could pass out. I keep thinking: *Please let him be OK. Please just let him be OK.*

Finally we arrive at the medical centre, and I watch as they wheel out a stretcher and lift him onto it. I have to kick off my skis to follow them in so it's a minute before I can locate him. Two medics are leaning over him, and he's shivering uncontrollably.

'I'm freezing,' he keeps saying. 'It's so cold in here.'

'It's fine – it's just shock. You're going to be OK. We'll give you something for the pain.'

'I don't want anything,' he says.

'Nothing too strong. Just fentanyl and a little bit of morphine.'

That sounds strong. But then I realise he was trying to make a joke. Boy doesn't make a sound as the needle goes in, but he gazes around as if he's looking for something. I come close and hold his hand. He grips it tightly.

The injection seems to calm him down, and they wheel him towards an X-ray machine.

The X-ray technician – who looks very young – stares

at the screen. As the picture emerges, a look of horror crosses his face.

'Oh ... *Das sieht aber schlimm aus*,' he says to his colleague.

'What does that mean?' Boy says. 'That's bad, right? What's happened?'

'Nothing!' says the X-ray guy. 'Try to relax, OK? Let's have some music!' And he turns on a radio, which starts playing 'Angels' by Robbie Williams.

'That's *all* I need,' mutters Boy. His face contorts and then all at once, his eyes close and he's fainted.

They swoop down, put an oxygen mask on him, and start wrapping him up. He's still not moving.

'We're taking him to the hospital in Innsbruck,' the paramedic woman tells me. 'Do you want to come with us?'

'Oh! Yes – only . . . OK.' Mum and Ed will be expecting me to be back around now.

But I hurry into the ambulance as the doors close. What was I thinking? As if it matters that I'm late home, when Boy is being driven away in an ambulance, sirens blaring. Especially since – although I bet nobody will *say* this – his accident was my fault.

29

Boy stays passed out in the ambulance, which means that I can phone Mum without disturbing him.

'Hi love, how is your day going?' she asks cheerfully. 'We've had a bit of a spill here. Josh skied into a big snowdrift and got drenched—'

'Mum, hang on – I can't talk for long. I'm with Boy and there's been an accident. We're on our way to the hospital.'

'Oh, no! What kind of accident?'

'He's broken his leg, I think. It's bad. He's unconscious.'

'I'll come and find you,' Mum says. 'Are you OK?'

'I'm fine. Nothing happened to me. It was just him—' I can feel my throat closing up. I have to swallow a few times before I can give her the name of the hospital.

'Don't worry, sweetheart. I'm sure he's going to be OK. Hang in there. I'll see you soon.'

When we get to the hospital, a nurse comes to meet

us, and they wheel Boy through corridors full of signs I don't understand. *Empfang. Kardiologie. Notfallmedezin.* It all adds to the surreal feeling. They take him between two swinging doors, and someone tells me to stay behind, in a waiting room. I sit down in a daze, still in my ski-boots. I have no idea where my skis are.

Forty-five minutes crawl by. Then Mum texts to say she's in the reception area. I run downstairs and practically fling myself into her arms. I'm so pleased to see her, I don't even care that she's wearing her embarrassing leather-look jeggings.

'I'm so sorry, darling,' she says. 'How is he?'

'I don't know. They've taken him away for another X-ray.'

Mum insists on me having a cup of tea and some chocolate from a vending machine, while I tell her what's happened. I don't tell her how I made Boy take the short-cut, though. I'm too ashamed.

'Have you been in touch with anyone else?' she asks. 'We could ring Tara. Or Gus. He's the resort manager; I've got his number.'

I let Mum take over and make calls. She might be over-dramatic, and a worrier, but it has to be said, she's great in a crisis.

'Right,' she says, hanging up. 'Gus is going to call the ski school, who will cancel his classes and spread the word among his friends. What about his family? Do we know how to get in touch with them?'

'Not really,' I admit.

'Hm,' she says. 'Well, let's not panic. We'll see what the doctors say.'

We go back to the waiting room, but there's no sign of any of the doctors from earlier. We ask everyone we can find but nobody seems to know who we're talking about. And I can't even give them his real name.

'What if they've lost him?' I ask Mum.

'Of course they haven't lost him,' she says. But she looks uneasy.

Finally I flag down a nurse I recognise. She tells me Boy has been taken to room 337.

'Do you want me to come with you?' Mum asks me.

'No thanks. I'd rather see him on my own.'

And to my slight surprise, she says 'Of course.'

30

I find Boy lying in bed, awake but miserable. He has a tube in his nose, and a drip in each arm, and he's wearing a hospital gown. His leg is bandaged from knee to ankle and propped on a pile of pillows on the end of the trolley.

'How are you?' I ask, softly.

'I don't know. I haven't seen the X-rays,' he says. 'I don't know if they're going to operate, or what the break is like. I haven't spoken to anyone or met a consultant – nothing.' I can see tears at the corners of his eyes. 'I don't know when I can go home. Or if I'm going to walk out of here again.'

Weirdly, seeing him frightened makes it easier for me to be calm.

'Of *course* you will! Don't even think that. You're going to be fine.'

I take his hand, and squeeze it. He looks a fraction better.

'What about you? How are you getting back to the resort?' he asks.

'My mum is here. She called the ski school, by the way.'

'Tell them I'll be back as soon as I can. Maybe in a few days.'

I have a feeling it's going to take longer, but I don't say that. 'Mum also asked me if you'd like us to call your family.'

'Oh . . . no, it's fine. I'll call them tomorrow, when I know more.'

His face contorts.

'What is it?' I ask, alarmed. 'Is it the pain?'

He nods. He's as white as a sheet, and his forehead is damp.

'I'll call a nurse.' I'm already at the door when he says, 'Stop. Don't. They'll just give me morphine. They've left me this—' he holds up a small clicking thing, 'to top it up, but I don't like taking things.'

I'm wondering whether I can click the thing for him without him noticing, when a nurse walks in and asks us something in German.

'No problem,' she says in English, when she sees our blank faces. 'I'm Karin, I'm on duty tonight. How is the pain? Are you pressing your morphine button?'

He says nothing. I catch the nurse's eye and discreetly shake my head. She tuts.

'You *have* to take your morphine. Because if you let the pain get too bad, then it will be too hard for us to control. Don't be a hero. OK?'

He doesn't reply, and a second later I see him clicking his button.

'Now rest. You'll need some sleep before your surgery tomorrow.'

His eyes fly open. 'Tomorrow? But I haven't even – what are they doing? I haven't even seen my X-rays.'

'The surgeon will be in tomorrow morning to explain it all to you.'

Once she's gone, we sit in silence for a while.

He laughs, weakly. 'I was just thinking. After all the crazy things I've done . . . I end up breaking my leg on a tiny, flat snowfield.'

'But it was my fault. I'm so sorry.'

'How do you mean?'

'I shouldn't have made you take that short-cut. Just because I was too chicken—'

'Stop it.' His voice is suddenly stronger. 'Don't ever say that. Don't even think it. I'm responsible for what I do on the mountain. Nobody else. OK?'

He looks so fierce and proud that all I can do is nod.

'Visiting time is over,' the nurse says again, popping her head around the door.

Visiting time's not the only thing that's over. I can't believe that this is how it ends.

'Goodbye,' I say. 'Good luck. I'll – I'll be in touch, OK?'

I kiss him on the cheek and walk out of the room, my eyes blurring.

31

When I get downstairs, Mum is waiting, along with someone I don't know. Which is good because it prevents me from bursting into tears.

'Hi, I'm Gus,' he says, shaking my hand. He's not what I expected from a resort manager. He has a shock of blond hair that he keeps ruffling in different directions. He's pink-cheeked and a little tubby, and wearing red chinos that he hitches up every so often.

'Hi, yeah, so, nightmare, huh? How is he?' he asks. 'Does he want, like, visitors?'

I explain Boy is sleeping now, and having surgery tomorrow.

'Yikes,' says Gus. 'I should speak to his father. I tried the number in his file but there's no reply, and it's basically, like, a landline. Who even rings a landline anymore? Like, if I'm going to make a call, I want to talk to a person, not a building?'

'Sure,' I say, wondering if he can possibly be for real.

'So if he's having major surgery, and his family doesn't even know about it, that's quite awkward really.'

'Mm,' says Mum.

'He said he'd call his family himself,' I say.

'Okey-cokey. Well, if he's asleep, I may as well hit the road,' Gus says, and we all turn to walk back outside. 'I shouldn't even be here but the ski school have pushed this on me. Which is ridiculous. I mean, I'm not that good at having awkward conversations, believe it or not.'

'No,' says Mum, catching my eye and giving me a tiny smile. It shouldn't be funny but it is, and I know she's going to do a brilliant impression of Gus later.

'But, you'll be able to stop by and visit him at least,' Mum says. 'Maybe tomorrow?'

'Yeah, no, sure, of course,' Gus says. 'I mean, I will do my genuine best, but I am having a Nightmare on Elm Street. One of our drivers has sprained his ankle in the Jacuzzi and I'm down a chalet assistant. I've got a new one but she can't start for another week.'

'Oh,' says Mum. 'Sounds stressful.'

'It is,' Gus frowns. 'Oh. I forgot you were guests for a minute. Soz.'

'It's fine,' Mum assures him. 'Just keep us posted about Boy.'

'Can I have your number as well?' I ask Gus, suddenly.

As we get into our car, I think about Boy waking up on his own, after having his surgery. There's no way his family can get here by tomorrow. And I don't really think he has anyone else.

That's when the most unlikely thought starts to take shape. Gus is down a chalet assistant for the next week.

So they'll need a temporary replacement. Maybe . . . that replacement could be me?

32

Our journey home is quiet. Mum is concentrating on the car and listening to the GPS – she doesn't like driving at the best of times. I'm busy pondering what might be the most insane idea I've ever had.

On the one hand, it seems like the perfect solution. But it's also daunting. I've never been away from my family – unless you count the Year Ten school trip to Paris, which was a) only three days and b) with the whole school. I don't know where I would stay, or if I could even do it.

Anyway, I would never be allowed to miss the second week of the holidays. I've got study to do. So there's no point even asking.

'You OK, Juno?' Mum asks, as we arrive back in the village. 'You look miles away.'

'Oh – yeah, I'm fine. Just tired.'

She parks in a wild diagonal beside our chalet. As she

turns off the engine, I notice that her hands are shaking. She wipes them on her jeggings before pulling the key out of the ignition.

'Mum!' I say suddenly, aware of what has just happened. 'You hate driving at night! You could have sent Ed, couldn't you?'

'I could. He offered. But I wanted to come.'

I reach out and give her a hug. 'Thank you.'

'That's OK. I was happy to do it,' she says, her face muffled in my hair.

And then it all clicks into place. Mum was scared of driving, but she loves me so she did it anyway. And I'm going to do the same for Boy.

33

'How is he?' Ed asks, as soon as we're in the door.

As Mum fills him in on the details, I sit down and slowly take off my ski-boots. My feet are aching and stiff after wearing them for so long. I'd like to change out of my ski-suit but I'm too exhausted, so I just strip down to my leggings and thermal top.

'Ouch,' Ed winces, when she's finished. 'Poor kid. That doesn't sound good.'

'It is miserable. Especially with him so far from home,' says Mum. She strokes my hair. 'I'm sorry you have to leave him like this, Ju. At least he's in good hands.'

I take a deep breath.

'Actually, Mum, I've got an idea. I could stay for the rest of the week, and come home next weekend.'

'Oh, Juno, I wish you could,' she says absently, standing up. 'Anyone want a cup of tea?'

She obviously isn't listening. Well, maybe I should

put my money where my mouth is and then ask her.

'I'm just making a phone call.' I pull my coat back on and run outside.

Standing on the porch, I dial Gus's number – quickly, before I lose my nerve.

'Oh, hi Juno.' There's music in the background and he sounds distracted, which makes me even more nervous. 'What's up?'

'I just wondered – you know the way you're down a chalet assistant? Maybe I could help? I've already done it. I helped Tara.'

'Yes, cool, I remember. But – sorry. You're leaving tomorrow, no?'

'Yes, but I could stay. For another week.'

'Oh.' There's a pause. 'What do your parents say?'

'I haven't asked them yet,' I admit. 'But I think they will say yes. If I have a job and somewhere to stay.' I'm not at all sure they will, but I won't worry about that yet.

'How old are you?'

'Seventeen,' I say, in trepidation. This will probably be a deal-breaker. I have no idea what the rules are but all the other chalet staff are at least eighteen.

But he says, 'In that case I would need your parents to sign something. Could you start tomorrow?'

'Yes!' Gus is talking about my responsibilities, the hours, and the pay – one hundred and fifty euros. It seems too good to be true.

'So this is a bit unusual,' he finishes. 'I wouldn't do it

except that I am totes desperate. And it makes my life easier if you can visit Boy.'

'Thank you! Thank you so much!'

'I'll put you in the same chalet as Tara. She'll show you the ropes, OK? Enjoy.'

And he hangs up. That's it. I stare at the phone, trying to process what just happened. I have a job. A temporary job, but still. He didn't even ask me what my predicated grades are!

Now all I need to do is convince Mum.

Back inside, Mum and Ed are sitting by the fire. They stop talking when I walk in.

'Who were you calling, Juno?' Mum asks. She can obviously sense something's up.

I take a deep breath. 'I want to stay here. Just for another week.'

'On your own? Juno, you're crazy! That is out of the question.'

'Please hear me out,' I plead. 'Gus has offered me a job for one week, as a chalet assistant. I'd be living with Tara, in a hostel. I get all my food and somewhere to stay and a hundred and fifty euros. It's just for a week,' I repeat. 'I promise I'll get as much study done here as I would at home – almost. And I'd be near to Boy. Please?'

'But – you just – I can't even –' Mum turns to Ed. 'Ed . . . help me, please?'

'Sorry, Siobhan,' Ed stands up. 'Not my business. This is between you two, and Juno's dad.'

He squeezes her shoulder and smiles at me, before

155

going upstairs. Mum tells me, 'Wait here,' and runs after him. I hear talking upstairs: his voice firm and low, hers more agitated. Five minutes later she reappears, trying to look calmer.

'Juno,' Mum says, sitting down opposite me and taking my hands in hers. 'I know you're upset. And concerned for Boy. But he's in the best place; people are looking after him. He will be fine. In any case, this isn't your responsibility. That's for his family, and his close friends.'

'But his family aren't here. And I don't know when they're going to turn up. His friends will probably drop by, but I could go there every day, after work.'

'But what about your revision?'

'Well,' I pause and play my trump card. 'I *might* have smuggled some coursework here with me.'

'Did you? Juno! Well—' But Mum shakes her head. 'No. Even if you did get any study done, you'd be all distracted for months to come ... I don't want to see your life turned upside down and your exams disrupted over a boy.'

I'm tongue-tied with frustration, trying to form a reply. Then, like a problem in maths, the contradiction in her argument suddenly becomes clear.

'Mum, why did you marry Ed?'

'What's that got to do with anything?' she asks, bewildered.

'You're talking about my exams being disrupted – but what about the fact that I've had to move house, and live with a new stepfather and two stepbrothers, all less than a year before my A levels?'

'That's totally different,' she says, defensively. 'Ed and I are adults. And we'd known each other much longer than a week when we got married.'

'Well, you didn't have to get married so soon – did you? You could have waited.'

'Juno, there were all sorts of considerations – financial ones, things to do with the boys – that meant it was sensible getting married when we did.'

I picture Mum on her wedding day. I think about the Sixties-style cream mini-dress she wore, and her bouquet of sweet peas, and the lunch reception afterwards. She didn't stop smiling the whole day.

'But you didn't get married because it was sensible. You were madly in love.'

She opens her mouth, then closes it.

'You're right, Ju,' she says. 'We were. We are. I'm sorry if it's been hard on you.'

'It's OK,' I murmur. But I'm glad that I said what I did. We've never talked about it before – not quite like that.

'Ed said I should let you stay,' she admits.

'*Did* he?'

'Yeah. Just now. He said I should let you grow up a bit.'

How amazing. Good for Ed.

'But where does it end, Ju? That's what worries me. You have your A levels . . .'

'I'm not stupid, Mum. I know I have my A levels. I only want to stay here for a week. One week.'

'Aargh.' Mum clutches her head in her hands again. I do feel guilty – she looks so stressed – but I don't back down.

'I could ask Dad?'

'No. I've got to decide this for myself,' says Mum.

'Or maybe you've got to let me decide.'

She looks up, her face pink from where she's pressed her hands against it.

'Mum, remember when you used to make me do stuff to spread my wings?' I smile at her tentatively. 'That's what I want to do now. Just for a week.'

After a long, long pause, Mum sighs. 'Fine. One week. But absolutely no longer.'

'Seriously?'

'Provided you ring me every day – and keep up your study as much as possible. I'll change your flights, and you can pay me back out of your wages and your birthday money.'

'Thank you, Mum.'

She gathers my hair into a ponytail again. 'I hope Boy knows how lucky he is to have you.'

As she pulls me into a hug, I start crying properly, partly out of relief that I can stay, and partly because I'm picturing Boy alone in hospital, and I don't think he's lucky at all.

34

'So,' says Tara next morning, when I come down for breakfast, 'I hear you're joining The Firm?'

'What firm?' asks Henry, looking up from his Coco Pops – a rare treat on our last day.

I let Ed explain what's happening.

'Well,' Tara says, 'obviously I am incredibly sorry that Boy's broken his leg ... But. Silver lining for me! It's going to be a massive, massive help. Do you know where the HQ is, to do all the paperwork and stuff? It's a little out of town so you might want to get a lift.'

Ed grabs his keys. 'I'll take you. I've got a couple of errands to run anyway.'

As I get into the car, I realise it's the first time I've been alone with him for any length of time. But it's not too awkward. We talk about Boy's accident and how I'm going to get to the hospital to see him. Ed tells me there's a bus, which I'm very glad about – though I feel stupid for not finding out myself.

'By all accounts it's an excellent hospital,' he adds.

'I hope so.' I look out of the window and sink back into worry.

'Just out of interest: is Boy dyslexic?' Ed says.

I turn to him in surprise. 'Yes, he is! How did you guess?'

'The other night, when you were playing cards, I noticed you helping him with the words,' he says. 'And I am, too. Dyslexic, I mean.'

'Oh! I didn't know that.' Though now that I come to think of it, I have seen some eccentric spelling from Ed – it took him ages to get the hang of Mum's name, and I once saw him write a note to himself to buy 'lite bubs'.

'No reason why you should,' says Ed. 'I get by. Dictation is a wonderful thing.'

This is interesting. But before I can ask him more, we've arrived at the office.

Luckily, Gus hasn't decided he made a terrible mistake by hiring me. He appears calmer than yesterday. His hair is flatter and he's not hitching his red trousers up quite so much.

'I had a call from the hospital,' he says. 'Boy's gone in for his surgery. I gave them your number and said they should call you when he comes out. And here's the doctor's number, and the ward details.'

'Oh! Sure.' As I take the doctor's number I start to

realise, for the first time, what a responsibility I'm taking on. Not to mention all the 'house rules' and other information Gus is giving me, too.

'Now. I do need one of your parentals to sign this,' Gus says, passing me a form.

I look up in consternation. 'I totally forgot. My mum's not here. My stepdad drove me.'

'That's fine, stepfather works.'

'Really?' I'm about to explain that Ed's not related to me, not really – but Gus obviously thinks he is. So Ed comes in and signs the form. It feels very weird – as if he's signing something that makes us officially part of a family. But, sitting in the car on the way home I decide, for the first time, that perhaps that's not the worst thing ever.

'Oh no!' I say suddenly, as we drive past the ski-hire place.

'What?'

'I've just remembered – I lost my skis yesterday. I was in such a state, I think I left them in the medical centre, after Boy's accident.'

'Don't worry,' he says calmly. 'They're probably still there – let's go and see.'

And he drives me to the medical centre where, sure enough, my skis are waiting for me in an office. Feeling one-part stupid and two-parts grateful, I load them in the back of Ed's car.

'Thanks for that,' I say, as the chalet comes into sight. 'And for taking me to the office.'

'That's OK.' There's a pause and then he adds awkwardly, 'Juno—'

'Yes?' I say, feeling embarrassed but also wanting to know what he's going to say.

'I know you didn't want to come skiing,' he says. 'But I'm glad you did. I hope it's been OK. Aside from Boy's accident, obviously.'

'No, it was good. I'm glad I came, too.'

I smile at him shyly, because I think we both know we're not just talking about skiing.

Inside, I expect Mum to ask questions about how it went and what my chalet duties are going to be. But she's busy rushing around finishing her packing, and chivvying the boys.

'I can't find my green sock,' Henry says, trailing through the hallway. 'It's my favourite.'

'Dad? Can I get my hair cut like Naymar?' Josh asks.

Ed's looking at his phone with a frown. 'Not now . . . Josh!' he says. 'I've had an email from your aunt. She says she's had a postcard from you . . . asking for help?'

So Josh *did* figure out how to post his card. I smile and tiptoe away from the resulting commotion, heading upstairs to pack my own stuff.

All too soon, we're gathering in the hallway to say goodbye.

Mum gives me a big hug. 'Text me,' she says. 'And call your dad. I've told him what's happening but you should talk to him too.'

Ed reaches into his pocket and hands me something.

'You can have this if you want, for Boy. It's an old MP3 player. It's got some audiobooks, and you can subscribe to podcasts and things. He might find it handy.'

I look at it, and before I have a chance to think, I give him a hug. I look at Mum, braced for her to start clapping or something, but she's distracted with the boys.

'Josh and Henry, why don't you show Juno the card you made?' she says.

Their card shows a ghastly-looking Boy in bed, with his tongue out, and two sinister figures with knives in their hands, though Henry explains it's 'medicine'. I tell them both, sincerely, that Boy will love it. Josh also makes the ultimate sacrifice and hands over his pack of Top Trumps cards.

'Hey, Juno,' he whispers loudly in my ear. 'You can be in our club.'

'You forgot to tell her the password,' says Henry. He leans forward and hisses, 'ROTTEN HAMSTER SKULLS.'

'Got it. OK, go, or you'll miss your flight.'

One forgotten charger, two trips to the loo and another hug from Mum, and they're on their way. As I watch Ed reverse the Mercedes down the drive, I have a mad impulse to run after them and tell them I've changed my mind. But it's too late now.

35

The next few hours are a blur of cleaning, vacuuming, polishing, and stripping beds. The work is back-breaking, but it's also a good distraction from worrying about Boy. He's now been in surgery for – I look at my watch – four hours.

'OK, I think we're done!' says Tara, straightening up. 'Let's lock up and I'll take you over to your new abode. Be warned, it's not exactly the Ritz.'

The chalet accommodation is only ten minutes' walk, but it's a world away from our cosy chalet: bare and functional, with lino floors and green walls. Tara tells me there are lots of Austrian students and backpackers there, but the chalet staff can be distinguished by their Ugg boots, leggings and Jack Wills jumpers. The place smells of hairspray and deodorant.

'I don't suppose you've got flip-flops or shower

shoes? Never mind,' Tara says, showing me the grim communal showers.

Our room consists of four metal bunk beds and a sink. I'm nervous at the idea of sharing a room with two people I've never met. What if one of them steals all my stuff, or shaves my eyebrows off while I'm asleep?

But Sophie and Jemima, when they come in from their morning shift, don't look as if they have enough energy to steal anything. They nod hello at me before collapsing on their beds, looking at their phones.

'Changeover day,' Sophie explains. 'It's exhausting.'

Sophie is pretty, with long pale hair and big pointed ears, like an elf. Jemima is attractive too, but more like a hobbit: short and dark and square. She rests on her bed for about two seconds before flinging herself off and changing out of her uniform into ski gear.

'Do you need SJ's uniform?' Jemima asks me. 'She left it under her pillow.'

'Thanks.' I reach for it tentatively and find it, as described. At least it's clean.

'Just out of interest . . . do you guys know *why* SJ left?' I ask.

'She said the altitude gave her headaches,' Jemima says, vaguely.

'And she was developing a wheat allergy from all the toasted sandwiches,' says Sophie. 'But I think she was just sick of being here.' She sighs. 'You can understand why, really. I can't remember the last time I left the village.'

'Her loss is our gain!' says Tara. 'Come on down, and we'll explore the wonders of the canteen.'

As we head downstairs, we pass Millie and her gaggle of friends on the stairs, all laughing and shoving each other. It occurs to me that they might not even know about Boy's accident.

'Excuse me,' I say, stopping beside Millie. 'I just – did you know Boy is in hospital?'

A guilty silence falls on the group.

'Yeah, we did and we're all quite stressed out about it.' Millie frowns, as if I'm somehow to blame.

'Yah, nightmare, how is he?' asks one of the boys, looking genuinely concerned under his Harry Styles hairdo.

'He's having surgery right now.'

'Give him my love,' says another girl. She bites her lip. 'I'd come and see him, but . . . I don't have a car.'

'And there's no way we could get the time off work,' Millie adds accusingly.

'OK,' I mutter. It's probably just as well. The sight of Millie at the end of his bed would probably finish Boy off anyway.

36

After days of sunshine, it's started snowing again and the sky is grey and heavy. As I stare out of the bus window on my way to the hospital, I watch the landscape change from Alpine cuteness to a sort of wintry dystopia. Bleak, slushy motorways. Signs in German that I don't understand. I have a history book with me but I've read the same paragraph about spinning jennies three times.

One of the doctors called me last night to say that Boy was out of surgery. Apparently the operation took seven and a half hours. I don't know anything about operations – I've never even had stitches – but that can't be good. I'm so worried about him that I don't even have the energy to fret about whether this is the right bus or if it's stopping in the right place.

Boy is in the same room as before, looking very sleepy and full of tubes. Gazing down at him, I'm reminded of a nature documentary I saw once, with a brown bear that had been captured for some kind of veterinary treatment. That's how he looks: huge, miserable, out of his element.

'How are you feeling?' I ask quietly, when he opens his eyes.

'I feel . . . fantastic,' he says croakily, with a slow smile.

'Are you serious?'

'Yeah. I feel A-OK.' After a long pause he says, 'How are you?'

'I'm fine.' He's obviously so out of it that he's forgotten that I'm not meant to be here. 'I'm working as a chalet assistant.'

'That's great,' he mutters, eyes half-closed. 'I really think that's excellent. You'd be so good at it.'

Gosh. I'd love to ask him why he thinks that but just in time, I remind myself that I'm not here to fish for compliments.

'You're so pretty and nice,' he continues dreamily. 'And you care about all the people in the world.'

He turns and widens his eyes at me, slowly, and then closes them again.

'That's what cats do,' he continues. 'You should never stare a cat right in the eye. It's very threatening. But they like it when you give them a slow blink.' He smiles, and I can't help giggling.

'Josh and Henry made you a get-well card,' I say. 'I know it looks a bit mad but . . .'

I hold it up for him to see.

'It's beautiful,' he murmurs, with another faraway smile.

Beautiful? Is he serious? It's more like the work of two underage killers. I'm wondering whether to leave when the nurse – the same one as yesterday – prods him awake, so she can take his temperature and blood pressure.

'I was asleep,' he complains.

'I'm sorry, but we have to keep waking you up. To make sure you recover from the anaesthetic.' She also checks his leg, which is packed with ice to reduce the swelling.

'Do you know how the operation went?' I ask her quietly, once his eyes have closed again. 'I still don't understand why it went on for so long.'

'I'm not sure,' she says. 'The surgeon will be here tomorrow morning, so you can ask him then.'

My heart sinks. I can't come until after lunch, but the surgeon is hardly going to rearrange his rounds for me.

'He seems very . . . happy though?'

She laughs. 'That's the drugs.'

After Karin leaves, Boy dozes some more. Looking at him, I think I understand why most people don't care about the environment or climate change or war in faraway countries. It's because, when you love someone this much, it feels as though nothing else matters. Right now, I'd burn a million units of carbon if it meant Boy could walk out of here.

'Juno?' he says eventually, opening his eyes.

'Yes?'

'Thanks for coming.' He reaches for my hand, and I feel so overwhelmed that I don't know what to do about it.

'Will you come and see me again?' he asks drowsily, as I stand up to leave.

'Of course. I can't come in the morning, but as soon as I can – lunchtime.'

As I walk out, I notice that the other rooms I pass are full of visitors bringing cards and balloons. Boy's room, with its one card from Josh and Henry, looks pretty bare in comparison.

37

It's getting dark by the time the bus arrives back in the resort. Pulling my black coat tightly round me, I think about Boy waking up tomorrow by himself, while I'm serving toast and scrambled eggs to the new guests. He'll be on his own when the surgeon comes by to update him on how the operation went. What if he's too groggy to understand it? Or worse – what if he does understand it, and it's bad news?

I'm so busy brooding that it takes me a while to hear that someone's calling my name.

'Juno. Juno! Juno!'

A dark-haired figure in a Puffa gilet is scampering up to me.

'Hi, are you Juno?' she says, breathlessly. 'I'm Tabitha. I heard about Boy. How is he?'

'Oh! He's OK. I think. I don't know.' My mind should be on more important things but I can't help noticing how pretty she is. Not model pretty, but in a girl-next-door way that's almost worse. 'He was sort of out of it.'

She wipes her nose with the back of her hand – the kind of gesture you can only get away with if you're very secure about your looks. 'So he can have visitors? I might go and see him tomorrow morning.' She pauses. 'If that's OK, I mean.'

Somehow I know she means 'if that's OK with you', not 'if that's OK with the hospital'. So she's nice as well as pretty. Why does that make me feel worse?

'Of course.' I give her the details about the hospital. At the same time I'm thinking: how come she's so keen to see him? But I squelch the mean thought. They're friends.

'The bus leaves from just here,' I add, pointing.

'I don't need a bus, thanks – I'm a driver, actually.'

'Oh. Right.' I thought she was a chalet assistant, like me. A driver: how grown-up.

'So are you, like . . . a guest here?' she asks, her brow furrowed.

I explain, and she smiles. 'Awww. That's so nice of you! You must really like him, to spend a week pulling hair out of plug holes!'

'Mmm.'

She gives a funny, hiccupping laugh. 'And, like . . . cleaning baths and mopping floors!'

I don't think she's doing it out of malice; she's clearly one of those people who finds lots of things hilarious.

I'm about to say goodbye when I remember about the surgeon coming by tomorrow.

Someone should be there, and if it can't be me then it has to be her.

'No probs,' she says. 'I'll make a note of what he says. I'm off to study biology next year so that's quite useful, isn't it? It'll be good practice!'

'Oh!' My impression of Tabitha as being a bit ditsy is suddenly flipped on its head. 'Where?'

I'm picturing somewhere like The International School of Snowboarding so I'm stunned when she says 'Cambridge!'

'That's great.' I hope I don't look as freaked out as I feel. She's got amazing eyelashes, and an adorable gap between her front teeth, and she's going to Cambridge. Quite frankly, *I* would go out with her.

38

Our new guests are two French families, with one son and four daughters between them. It's so strange to be serving them breakfast just like Tara used to serve us, and even stranger when I hear one of the daughters, who's about my age, tell Tara she's scared of skiing.

'You'll be fine,' I tell her with a smile, as I carry the breakfast dishes towards the kitchen. 'If I can do it, anyone can do it.'

I had intended to put on fresh clothes and do my make-up before my trip to the hospital. But the dishwasher goes gritty so I have to wash things up by hand, and I end up making a run for the bus while still in my shorts and black T-shirt. While I'm on the bus, Mum texts to wish me a Happy Easter. I can't help thinking this is the strangest Easter I've ever spent.

When I get to Boy's room, he seems miles better than yesterday – still full of tubes, but much more alert.

'I'm OK,' he says, when I ask him how he's feeling. 'Just – knackered. And my throat is really sore.' He frowns. 'Wait. Juno, what are you doing here? I thought you went home!'

'I'm filling in for a week, as a chalet assistant. I told you yesterday.'

'You were *here* yesterday?'

'Yes! You were a bit woozy, though.'

'I can't believe you stayed.'

He's staring as if he's never seen me before. Does he think it was weird of me to stay? Too clingy, or something? To hide my confusion, I ask quickly, 'So what did the surgeon say?'

'Nothing, he hasn't come by yet.'

'OK!' I'm so relieved I didn't miss him. 'By the way – Happy Easter! I got you some chocolate. I looked everywhere for Kinder eggs, but they were all out of them.'

'Don't worry. Tabitha got me some.'

'Oh! That's good. Did – did she stay long?'

But Boy doesn't get a chance to tell me, because there's a knock at the door. It's the surgeon – trailed by various other doctors, one of whom is taking notes.

'How are you doing?' he asks Boy, cheerfully. 'You're famous in this hospital, so we've all come to have a look at you!'

Boy and I exchange looks. Whatever you want to be in a hospital, it's not *famous*, is it?

'Thanks – I'm OK,' he says. 'When can I ski again?'

I can't believe that was his first question. Well, actually maybe I can.

'First things first,' the surgeon says, sitting down beside the bed. 'You have what we call a spiral fracture. That means you broke your left tibia, but instead of snapping it clean, you twisted the bone until it shattered. So, to fix you up, we nailed all the little pieces onto a titanium plate.'

Boy is staring at his leg. 'So I've got a metal plate in there?'

'Yes. The good news is that you have no soft-tissue damage. Just the bone. And that's good, because the bone will heal, stronger than it was before.'

I immediately wonder what the bad news is, but Boy says, 'How do you think I did it?'

'I think your ski hit something under the snow – you were on deep powder snow? – and the ski stopped, but you kept turning.'

Boy nods. I feel another chill of guilt. I know Boy said that it was his decision to go off-piste, but I can't help feeling terrible about it.

'So, how long before I'm back to normal? I . . .' His voice trails off, as he looks at all the assembled doctors. 'I'm climbing Everest in June. I should be OK for that, right?'

They all exchange glances, as if to say: he doesn't get it, does he?

'I'm sorry, but no.' The surgeon leans forward, clasping his hands in front of him. 'After a week or so we will start you on crutches, then after about two months, you'll be able to put a little bit of weight on that leg. Maybe thirty per cent.'

'I'll be on crutches for two *months*?'

'More, probably. Three or four. It depends.' The surgeon continues, 'I may as well tell you that if you had this break in a developing country, they probably would have amputated the leg. Or they would have put it in a cast and you would never have walked again. So you see that it could be worse.'

He waits a second to let this sink in, then beams at us and says, 'But don't worry! You will be fine. What about your family?'

'I – yeah. They're coming soon.'

'Good. You will need help, every day, for the next three months at least.'

Boy nods, but I think he's stopped listening. He must be in shock.

The surgeon stands up. 'For now, you're here and we will take good care of you. Rest, and I'll see you again tomorrow.'

We're quiet after they've left. I'm in shock myself.

'I'm so sorry,' I say tentatively, after a while.

'Oh well. Sucks to be me,' he says lightly.

He doesn't fool me, though. He's clearly in pieces. If only I could think of something to say, but nothing comes to mind, so we sit in silence.

'When does your dad arrive?' I ask eventually.

'What? Oh.' He pauses. 'Saturday.'

'Not until Saturday? But – what if they discharge you before then? Where will you go?'

'Back home.'

'Back home where? Like, the garage?'

'Sure. Why not?'

'But . . . you heard what the doctor said, about you needing help—'

'Look, he has to say that,' Boy says impatiently. 'To cover himself. But I'll be fine. I can get a bus back to the village.'

'A *bus*?' He's still on a drip. Is he crazy?

'Fine, a taxi.'

I'm trying to picture this. Will Meribel be opening the door for him?

'But you won't be able to manage your bags, even! You'll need someone with you. I could come and stay with you, if you want?'

'No,' he says sharply. 'You don't have to worry about me.'

This makes no sense. How could I not worry about him? But before I can say anything, there's the sound of a text from Boy's phone.

'Where is it? I left it charging . . .' I'm horrified to see him shuffle sideways as if to hop out of bed for it.

'Wait!' I shriek. 'Don't move!'

'I can reach it!' But I beat him to it, and hand it over with a sinking feeling. I can tell, from his smile, who it is.

'It's Tabs. She says . . .' He puts the phone down,

looking exhausted. 'Actually, do you mind reading it?'

Taking the phone with my fingertips, I read out, '"What did the surgeon say? Blue slopes only for now?"' I add reluctantly, '"Xx."'

He smiles again. 'Can you reply? Just tell her … No, wait. Um … Just put, "Doc says crutches for three months. He reckons Everest is out but what does he know?" And then a smiley face. And a thumbs-up.'

'Do you want me to add an X?' I ask, coolly.

'No, it's fine,' he says, totally missing my sarcasm. I finish his stupid text and press send.

Then I feel bad. I don't want my visit to end on a sour note.

'Oh, I almost forgot.' I take out the MP3 player. 'I put some comedy podcasts on this, and a couple of audiobooks. Including Harry Potter. You're never too old for Hogwarts.'

I was looking forward to giving him this. I thought he would be really pleased. But he just says 'Thanks', and puts it on his table beside my chocolate.

'It's great,' he adds. 'But you don't have to spend your whole time here doing stuff for me.'

'I'm not.' I stand up to leave, my heart sinking even further as I hear another bleep; Tabitha must have texted him back. 'I have to go now anyway – my bus is leaving soon. Is there anything else you need?'

'I wouldn't mind a cigarette.'

'*What?*'

'I was joking,' he says wearily, picking up his phone. 'Thanks for coming.'

But he doesn't ask me when I can come back. And is it my imagination, or does he look . . . *relieved* that I'm leaving?

39

On the bus on the way back, I try to tell myself everything is fine. It's a bad injury, but Boy will be OK. But at the same time, I'm not sure how happy he is to have me here. Especially when he seems to be getting on better with Tabitha than with me. I can't help wondering if staying here might have been a mistake.

I want to ask Tara what she thinks, but our room is action stations. Tara's getting dressed up in a silky top and jeans; she's putting on make-up and everything. Jemima and Sophie are sitting on their beds, watching.

'What's going on?' I ask, sitting down.

Jemima turns round, looking excited. 'Tara is going on a date . . . with Jean-Philippe!'

'That's great! Who is Jean-Philippe?' I pull out my uniform and give it a discreet sniff, before spraying on some more Chance.

'He's the new pastry chef at the Aurora,' says Tara. 'He's very nice.'

'He is *smoking* hot,' adds Sophie.

'I swapped my nights out with Jemima. Hope that's OK,' Tara says.

'Of course! That's great!' I say, happy for her.

'Where's he taking you?' asks Jemima.

'Not sure yet.' Tara dabs on some more mascara. '*But* he's got a car, so maybe out of the village! Who knows?'

'You're so lucky,' says Sophie, sounding wistful. 'I *dream* about leaving the village.'

'You'll have to tell us *all* about it,' says Jemima.

I run downstairs, thinking maybe Emma will be around to Skype. I sent her a quick message explaining that I'm staying, but I haven't actually heard back from her yet.

As soon as I log on, I see that I have an abnormal number of messages. There's even one from Scarlett saying, *Juno, I've heard the news. I'm SO worried for you. This week will affect the REST OF YOUR LIFE.*

After staring at all the messages – all variations on *You OK babe?* and *Come home*, plus crying faces – I spot one from Emma saying, *I've sent you an email.*

Oh, no. I have a very bad feeling about this. I don't think Emma has ever emailed me before; it's like she's sending me an official letter of complaint, or something. I open her email with my heart in my mouth.

Hi Juno,

I'm so worried about you. Are you sure you're making the right decision? I know you really like Boy. But you can't throw your A levels away over him. I know you said it's only a week, but you can't afford to miss a week's revision, Juno. None of us can.

I've spoken to Ruby and Mia and they agree with me. Please come home! We miss you.

Lots of love,

Emxxx

I can't believe this! Emma of all people! I would have expected it from Scarlett, but for Emma to have a go at me . . .

Or is it me?

Suddenly I have a horrible feeling of doubt. Maybe Emma is right – maybe they're all right. What if I *have* done something stupid by staying? Especially considering the way Boy is acting now. I haven't done a minute's study yet, either.

There's another ping. It's Jack! I Skype him, and he says, 'Tell me *everything*.'

I give him the full story, right up to the intervention. To my relief, he definitely thinks I did the right thing, and that it's really romantic.

'But what about everyone else?'

'Ignore them. Our lives are so boring right now, we're desperate for any distraction.'

'You think?'

'Of course! By the time you get back, Mr Assworth will have worn his skinny jeans again, or there'll be a new latte flavour in Starbucks, and everyone will have forgotten it.'

I half-smile at the memory of the art teacher, Mr Ashworth, and his skinny jeans, which were the talk of the school for a week.

'So how is he?' Jack asks.

Sighing, I explain that Boy is OK, but he doesn't seem very keen to have me around.

To my surprise, Jack says, 'I think it's normal for him to push you away a bit. He's got his pride, you know? He probably wishes he could go into his man cave and lick his wounds, but instead he's stuck in a trolley bed in a gown that does up at the back. That's not a good look for anyone.'

'You're right, Jack! I bet that's exactly how he feels.'

'Give him some space, and he'll come running.' He pauses. 'Maybe not running but definitely *crutching* after you.'

This makes me laugh. Jack is always great at doing that.

'There's also this ex of his . . .' I explain about Tabitha, and how she seems to always know the right thing to say to Boy while I'm getting on his nerves.

But Jack dismisses this. 'Juno! The clue's in the name. She's the ex. She's history. OK?'

'OK,' I say, staring at my shoes and hoping that he's right.

40

Jemima's working with me tonight, and she persuades me to go to the Buddha Bar with her after we finish.

'Do you know Tabitha?' I ask her casually, as we walk to the bar.

'Tabitha? Of course! She's a legend.'

Ugh. I don't know why but whenever I hear someone described as a legend, I kind of instantly dislike them. Then I shake myself. Why am I blaming Tabitha for the way Boy is acting?

The Buddha Bar is as busy and heaving as ever. The noises and music are a good distraction; I'm suddenly glad I came out. As we queue for drinks, I decide Jack is right. The whole Tabitha thing is purely in my head. And I need to give Boy some space, that's all. This night out is a start.

Suddenly the lights flicker, and luminous dots appear on the walls. An amplified voice says, 'Happy

Easter! Tonight at the Buddha . . . It's Dice Night!'

'What's Dice Night?' I ask Jemima.

'Oh, it's one of their gimmicks. It's quite cool, actually. Every time you buy a round you roll a dice. If you get a double – any double – the round is free.'

'Yeah!' says Mikey, popping up next to us. 'So it makes sense to buy a huge round, in case you win big.'

I don't want to be stingy but the chances of scoring a double are tiny, so I buy a normal round. Sure enough, I roll a three and a one. I knew it. I bet people hardly ever win: that's what the bar is counting on.

'Oh, look,' says Jemima, as I hand her her drink. 'It's the Miltabs.'

'What?'

'Tabitha and Millie. That's their name for themselves.'

'I have a name for them and it's not Miltabs,' says Mikey.

Jemima laughs. 'Shh, they'll hear you.'

Tabitha comes straight over and Millie trails behind reluctantly.

'So how is he?' Tabitha asks me, crinkling her brow. 'Poor guy. Crutches for three months, huh?'

'Yeah, he's pretty devastated.'

'It's, like, a miracle that they've managed to keep him in hospital. I can see him crawling home and trying to fix his own leg with some sticks. Can't you?'

'I totally can!' I say, laughing despite myself.

'Can we join you?' Tabitha asks.

Millie looks horrified, but Jemima and Mikey are already scooting over to make room.

'So!' Tabitha says, leaning in towards me. 'I'm not going to be able to visit Boy tomorrow, but—'

Millie is tugging at her sleeve. 'Tabs? Tabs? Tabs?'

'What?' says Tabitha finally.

'I'm getting a drink,' says Millie. 'What do you want?'

'I'll have a B-52,' says Tabitha. 'Ooh, wait! It's Dice Night!' She pulls some notes out of her wallet. 'Get five of them!'

Millie puffs at her fringe and says the first reasonable thing I've heard out of her. 'I'm not going to roll a double, Tabs.'

'You never know!' says Tabitha. 'Give it a go!'

I suppose I shouldn't be shocked that this is Tabitha's attitude to Dice Night. She's a risk-taker as well as a fun-lover. No wonder Boy liked her.

Tabitha turns back to me. 'What was I saying? Oh yeah. I can't go tomorrow but I can drop by on Thursday.'

'Oh – good. That's great.'

She pauses, as if she's seen something in my expression. 'Hey. You know there is absolutely nothing between us, don't you?'

'Um, sure,' I say uneasily.

'It is *so* completely over,' she says. 'And it was never that serious. You know what it's like when you're thrown together in a tiny place like this for months on end.'

I don't, actually, but I nod.

'We had a lot of fun at the time. But then, he began to drive me insane . . . and not in a good way! I mean, that crazy garage . . . Those stairs! Like a horror film!'

'It is like a horror film,' I agree, smiling.

'I know he's saving for Everest or whatever – but honestly! I think he *prefers* living like a vagrant. Once we were walking along and he darted into the middle of the road to pick up a coin. He nearly got himself killed, for twenty cents!'

I don't *want* to laugh at any of this, but I can't help it; it sounds so familiar.

'Though we did have some good times,' Tabitha continues. 'He's so funny, isn't he? And he's such a good skier. I found that very sexy.'

'Mm,' I say stiffly.

She scrunches up her nose at me. 'Anyway . . . he's a sweetie. But so stubborn! I mean, look at the way he hasn't even told his family about his accident.'

'*What?*'

'You know,' says Tabitha. 'He's always had a weird relationship with his dad, but not to let him know that he's in hospital – it's nuts! But there's no telling him, is there?'

'No,' I whisper.

At that moment Millie reappears, with a tray of B52s. 'Wooohooo!' she shrieks. 'I rolled a double four!' She puts the shots in front of Tabitha, who distributes them among the rest of us.

'It just shows you!' Millie says smugly. 'Good things happen to good people!'

I can't reply. I can barely swallow my shot. Boy's father isn't coming on Saturday. He hasn't even told him he's in hospital. And he lied to me.

41

I'm not going to march into Boy's hospital room the next day and demand an argument. I'm too hurt. And humiliated, and confused about why he lied to me and told Tabitha the truth. In fact, I'm in two minds whether to go and see him at all. But I can't stay away.

'Oh, hi,' he says, glumly, when I walk in.

Not a great start. I put on my most cheerful voice and say, 'How are you? It's a beautiful day outside.'

'Yeah. A perfect skiing day.'

I know I probably keep saying the wrong things, but does he have to be so mean? I feel such a mess of love and anger and concern that I don't know which end is up. I just know that I can't keep quiet anymore.

'Why haven't you contacted your dad?' I ask him.

He picks up his phone and starts playing with it. 'Because . . . it's none of his business.'

I'm so relieved he didn't say 'It's none of your business.' Though he looks as if that's what he's thinking.

'Don't you think he'd want to know?'

He laughs. 'Sure, he'd want to know. So that he could say something like, "That was stupid, wasn't it?" And then breathe down my neck for months. No thanks.'

I'm sure he's exaggerating, but I don't push it. 'Couldn't you call one of your brothers then?'

Shaking his head immediately, he says, 'No. They've got their own lives. Hugh works all the time. And Theo's got a kid, and his wife is pregnant.'

'But they would still want to help you.'

'Well, I don't need help.'

I look at him: immobile in a hospital bed, full of tubes and drips, asleep half the day. He can't even stand up.

'Maybe while I'm here,' he corrects himself. 'But not when I'm out.'

'Of course you will! You can't carry things when you're on crutches. You can't make a cup of tea, or have a shower by yourself. You need people.'

'No, I don't.' His face is dark. 'I'm better on my own.'

'Is that what *Tabitha* thinks?' I ask, hating myself for saying this but unable to stop.

'It is, actually.'

'Why did you tell her about your dad – and not me?'

'Because I knew she'd be cool about it.'

This makes me wince. 'What do you mean – cool?'

'I mean, she thinks it's my decision. She's letting me do my own thing. She's not on my case.'

'You think I'm *on your case*?'

He shrugs.

I'm really alarmed at how quickly things between us have turned hostile. To try to lighten the atmosphere, I say, 'Look at any horror film. The ones who survive are the ones who band together. If you limp away from the group, the zombies will pick you off. That's just how it works.'

'Luckily this isn't a zombie film,' he says.

'Well, real life doesn't work like that either! We have to depend on each other.'

'Maybe I don't want to depend on anyone.'

Now I'm angry. 'But that's not fair on the people who want to help you! I want to help you! Otherwise why would I be here?'

He looks at me properly for the first time, and his expression is so cold and horrible, he barely looks like the same person.

'I never asked you to stay.'

Without a word, I start gathering together my stuff, and walk right out the door, not looking at him. He doesn't say anything, and I don't turn back.

42

I never asked you to stay.

The words ring in my head, all the way back to the resort, where I somehow manage to get upstairs to the room and curl up on my bunk bed, in a ball. I check my phone, once, but he hasn't called me and I'm not calling him again.

I wish I could cry, but I'm in a dry-eyed hell. I can't believe how much it hurts, and how humiliated I feel. What was I thinking? I should never, ever have stayed here. Suddenly I have a pang of homesickness so bad it makes me gasp. I would give anything to be at home with Mum and Ed and the boys. I didn't realise I thought of it as home but I suppose I do now.

After I don't know how long, Tara comes in, brushing snow off her shoulders. When she sees me, she frowns. 'Hey! What's happened? Is Boy all right?'

'Yeah. He's fine. But . . .'

I don't need to say any more. She can guess.

She sits beside me on the bed. 'I'm really sorry, Juno. It is the worst feeling in the world.'

'No it's not. What about people in earthquakes, or . . . or . . ?'

Tara just shakes her head, and repeats, 'It's the worst feeling in the world.'

I'm not going to argue. She's right.

'Listen, if it's any consolation – I'm really glad you stayed. Don't know how I would have managed without you.'

'Thanks,' I whisper.

Tara stands up. 'I hate to be a downer but you know we've got work in twenty minutes?'

'I'll be there,' I say, trying very, very hard to keep my voice steady.

I can't do it. I can't stay here, in the resort, and have everyone know that I overstayed my welcome, and that Boy has dumped me.

But somehow I get up, and straighten my uniform, and brush my hair, and then I go to the chalet. The mindless nature of the work helps a little. There's no way I could study right now. But I can cut up bread and smoked salmon, and unload the dishwasher, and polish glasses. I just wish I could go to sleep and wake up in London, without any memories of Austria, skiing or Boy.

43

The next day is the same as usual, until the end of the morning shift, when I mix it up a little. Instead of getting the bus to the hospital I go straight back to the hostel and lie on my bed. I check my phone, just once, but of course he hasn't called.

'You coming skiing?' Tara asks. 'I'm meeting the others at three thirty.'

'No, I'm going to study.' I pull out a book and wave it at her. But as soon as she's gone, I put it away and roll over.

Around two o'clock, I realise I've barely eaten anything since I left the hospital yesterday. Rolling off the bed, I drag myself down to the canteen. I manage to eat my Wiener schnitzel in peace, but on the way out, I almost trip over Millie and all her pals – minus Tabitha. Suddenly, I want to know the truth about her and Boy.

'Have you seen Tabitha? Is she at the hospital?' I ask Millie.

'She might be,' Millie says, looking down her nose at me. 'She's been giving Boy a *lot* of support lately.'

'Is that what they call it?' says one of her jock friends, and they high-five each other.

'Thanks.' Moving like a sleepwalker, I manage to get past her and upstairs, where I stumble onto my bed.

I don't know if they're back together; they might not be. But even if they're just friends, it still kills me that she understands him better, that he can talk to her but not me. I picture him saying *I knew she'd be cool about it*, and I want to die.

Help, I think desperately. I don't even know who I'm talking to; I just know I can't stand to feel like this for a minute longer. I can't call Emma; she wouldn't *say* 'I told you so' but she would think it. And I don't want to call Mum and admit that Boy's rejected me – not after begging her to let me stay. Fingers trembling, I call my dad.

'Hi, love,' he says. 'How is Austria?'

And of course, at the sound of his voice, I start to cry for the first time since I left the hospital. It's several minutes before I can tell him the whole thing, starting with meeting Boy and ending with him pushing me away.

Dad sighs. 'My poor little girl.' Which makes me sob again.

'Listen, Juno,' Dad says. 'I'm not going to tell you that

he's a little toe-rag who doesn't deserve my beautiful daughter. Because even though it's true, it wouldn't help, would it?'

'Not really.'

'Just try to remember: this is what's happening *now*. This is how you're feeling now. But it's temporary. It won't always be like this.'

It's easy for Dad to say that. He's a professional philosopher. 'But Dad – I can't bear it,' I gulp.

Then Dad says something that takes me by surprise.

'But you *are* bearing it, Ju. You're doing it.'

'Oh.' I hadn't thought of it that way, but it makes a strange kind of sense.

'I just feel so stupid,' I admit. 'It was a mistake to stay here.'

'Tell me more about it. What's it like there?'

I lean back and describe the view, from the pointed white roofs to the deep blue sky.

'Well. I don't want to make you jealous but I am looking out of the window at the rain, some litter and a pigeon eating a Pret a Manger sandwich.'

I wouldn't have thought I could laugh at anything today, but I do.

'You can do this, Juno.'

'Thanks, Dad,' I say, feeling tearful all over again.

We talk for another twenty minutes or so, and I hang up feeling much calmer. I think about what Dad said, about how I *am* bearing it. I always thought that if you could bear something it meant you didn't mind it. But now I understand. You mind it, but you keep on going anyway. Maybe it's just another way of being brave.

You can do this, Dad said. Who else said that? Oh. Boy.

Driving the thought of him away, I look out of the window. The sun is shining. The sky is the same pure, perfect blue. The mountains are Persil white. This time next week I'll be back in my hamster wheel of school-study-sleep. Do I really want to spend my last two days here curled up on a metal bunk bed?

On an impulse, I roll over and message Tara. 'Wait for me. I'm on my way!'

44

The others are waiting when I get there: Jemima, Sophie
and Lara. It's the lift where Boy and I met on our last
day, but I'm not thinking about that.

'Where's Tara?' asks Sophie. 'Did anyone hear how it
went with Jean-Philippe?'

'I forgot to ask her,' I say, guiltily. I've been too busy
brooding on my own problems.

'There she is!' Sophie starts hurling questions at Tara
while she's still half a slope away, but her face seems to
say it all.

'It was . . . bad,' she says, coming to a stop in front of
us.

'Bad how?' asks Jemima.

Tara shudders. 'It was all going fine – but then over
dessert, he started showing me his Instagram feed.'

'So?'

'He's got pictures of every cake he's ever made. He's been pastry-cheffing for seven years, so he's got thousands. And I had to look at *all of them*.' She looks traumatised. 'Some of them weren't even cakes. Some of them were just *buns*.'

This makes us all crack up.

'He showed you his buns!' says Lara.

'Don't,' says Tara, but she's laughing as well.

We glide off together, still chuckling. What with the laughing, and the company and the fresh air – I feel like a new person. Soon I'm chatting away to Lara about her degree course.

'I'd like to specialise in family law, or environmental law,' she tells me.

'Environmental law?'

'Yup. Protecting communities against development . . . taking legal action against power suppliers to make them greener, that kind of thing.'

I had never thought about this before. I'd never thought about law before, full stop. But this sounds fascinating. And the idea of doing something practical about the things that worry me makes me feel so much better.

I'm about to ask Lara another question when I see we've come to a bend in the slope that looks ominously familiar. The girls all surge ahead, but I hang back.

This is it. This is where Boy had his accident.

'Wait up,' Tara calls. 'Juno, what is it? Don't worry! You can do it.'

'Come on,' roars Lara, thirty feet below me. 'It's a baby slope.'

'It gets better after this stretch,' Jemima offers. Which is exactly what Boy said.

But he didn't get hurt here. He got hurt off-piste, because I was scared of this slope. I think of the irony; after all the dangerous things he's done, his accident happened in a field of powder snow.

And that's when it hits me: I could spend my whole life trying to avoid danger, but there's no guarantee that it will always work. In fact, it could end up making things worse. So I may as well try to be brave.

Taking a deep breath, I inch forward, snowploughing carefully from side to side. It's scary. But as I follow the others, wobbling like a baby penguin on ice, it gets easier. Until . . . it's actually *fun*. The slope's levelled out, we're flying: this is the fastest I've ever gone. And it feels fantastic!

'Wooooohooooooooooo!' I scream as we zip forward, gathering speed.

Speed, wind, air: this is magic. By the time we come to a halt, I'm on a high that's unlike anything I've ever felt before.

'You were so funny,' says Lara, swirling behind me and almost knocking me over. 'This was you.' And she does an impression of me that sounds more like a wolf howling.

We're all laughing now, and I don't care. I feel exhilarated. If I did that I can do *anything*. Including getting over Boy.

45

Next morning, a miracle occurs: I wake up feeling human again. I still don't want to think about Boy, but I find myself humming as I clean up after breakfast. I go skiing with the girls again after lunch, and the sight of Millie and Tabitha in the distance only makes me feel sick for a minute. And in the evening I make dinner by myself, for the very first time, while Tara sets the table.

'Are you sure?' I ask her for the millionth time, as I crumble together flour and butter. It's salmon *en croute* – salmon with a puff-pastry crust.

'Absolutely. I'm rubbish at pastry. Mine always turns out like Play-Doh – except you can eat Play-Doh, can't you?'

I've made pastry before, at home, but I'm still pretty nervous – this is the first time I've attempted a main dish here. But it comes out perfectly, all glossy golden brown, thanks to my signature egg-and-milk glaze.

'*C'est délicieux!*' says Martine, one of the mums.

'Yes, really delicious,' says the eldest and tallest daughter – Camille. 'What's your secret?'

'I have very cold hands,' I admit, and everybody laughs.

Tara and I are a well-oiled machine at this stage, so we've finished work and are heading home by nine. It's starting to snow now; the lighted windows all look so cosy and inviting.

'What do you want to do tonight?' says Tara. 'I feel like vegging out.'

'That sounds great.'

When we get back to the hostel, we find Sophie and Jemima in the common room with a couple of the other chalet assistants. It looks as if nobody's in the mood to go out. So instead we huddle under blankets, drinking hot chocolate and staring out as the windows whiten. I've got my laptop with me, and I was going to do some revision, but I end up looking up law courses, and environmental and public policy. There's so much more out there than I'd realised.

'Why don't we watch a film?' says Sophie. 'I know! *Pitch Perfect*?'

'Noooo,' says Jemima, clasping her hands over her ears. 'I can't take it, Sophie.'

But Sophie's already singing over her, and another girl, Felicity, joins in. Soon we're all singing – or in my case, laughing. Suddenly I think: I was a bit scared of all these girls initially but they're great. I feel as though they're my friends now. I thought the chalet work might be too hard, but it's not. *I can do it.* I still feel heartbroken whenever I think about Boy, but maybe this week hasn't been such a disaster after all.

It's funny. Emma and the girls thought it was a terrible idea to stay. Jack thought it was a great idea. I wasn't sure which of them I should trust, but now I know I have to trust myself. Maybe it was a mistake, but it was *my* mistake. And I'm making the best of it.

Looking back at my laptop, I bookmark a couple of uni courses that look interesting. I think I might actually do this. I might change my course.

Thinking of next year makes me think of school, and home, and my friends. Before I can chicken out of what will probably be an awkward conversation, I retreat into a quiet corner of the room and message Emma – just a quick *How's it going?* Then I send her a picture of me skiing.

She messages back with a load of exclamation marks and hearts. Then she asks, *Are you OK?*

Of course I'm OK. Thanks for your email, I type quickly. *I know you're just being concerned, but, Em, I have to make my own decisions.* I pause and then add, *It might not have been right for you but it was the right thing for me.*

I know. I'm sorry, she writes. *I was interfering. I didn't know the others were going to gang up on you like that.*

It's fine. Honestly. And it's true; I had almost forgotten it. So much has happened since then. *Also,* I write, *I never told you this, but I was banned from studying for the first week of these hols* anyway.

By who??

Ms K. So yeah. I'm avoiding burnout apparently.

I didn't know, Emma types. *I thought they WANTED us to burn out. How is Boy?*

He's OK, I think. Things are over with us though.

Oh no!!! I'm really sorry, she writes, adding a crying face and flowers. And I know she means it. *How are you feeling?*

I'm OK. I'm actually glad I stayed. I've had a taste of life after school.

AMAZE, she messages back. *WHAT IS THAT LIKE?!*

Looking around the common room at the girls laughing and the snow falling outside, I message back, *I think we're going to like it.*

46

After a long discussion the others have decided to watch *The Notebook*, but nobody can find the DVD.

'It must be up in our room,' says Jemima.

'I'll go and get it. I want to get my lip balm as well,' I say. I also had a missed call, no doubt from Mum; I should call her back. Despite her saying she wanted me to phone her every evening, we've only texted as I've just been too busy. And surprisingly, she's been fine with that.

As I go upstairs, though, I check my phone and see that the missed call is from a number I don't know. A local number. They've left a voicemail. As ever, this scares me. Is it the Austrian police? Have they discovered I'm here illegally, or something?

But it's not the police.

'Hi Juno, it's me.' Pause. 'I'm just ringing to say I'm sorry about everything. I know you probably don't want to hear from me again but . . . Yeah. I'm sorry.' There's another pause. 'Bye.'

The sound of his voice brings back such a wave of emotion that my heart races, my throat tightens, and my knees wobble so badly I have to sit down.

My first impulse is to call him back, immediately, and tell him it's all fine and ask him when I can see him again. But then I hesitate. He wants to say he's sorry – but about what? He could just be sorry for how he treated me. Sorry that he's back with Tabitha, even. He might just want to say goodbye, as a friend.

Five minutes ago I was feeling sane, sorted and even happy – now I'm a mess. If I call Boy, I'll be plunged back into uncertainty, maybe have my heart broken all over again. I can't reopen that wound. It's too scary, too overwhelming, too much to cope with. Boy said he was better on his own; well, maybe I am, too.

47

I'm sitting outside a café on the mountain – the same one I went to with Boy, but today I'm here with Jemima and Sophie, who've gone inside to buy our lunch while I guard our table. The sky is still a deep blue. I'm wearing sunglasses and I have an actual tan now – it's mostly freckles, but still.

It's my last day at the resort. The French family are going home tomorrow morning, and so am I. I can't believe how quickly the week has gone by. The only thing I haven't really done this week, if I'm totally honest with myself, is revision. But I still feel I've learned an awful lot.

Hearing a buzz, I see I have a text from Mum. *Can't wait to see my chalet girl. Will be at arrivals when you land. I'm so proud of you!*

I text back, *Can't wait to see you too xxx*

I haven't mentioned Boy the last few times we've

texted, and somehow I think Mum knows not to ask. I was dreading telling her about it. I begged her to let me stay because of him, and look what happened. But now I feel differently. I am sad that it ended, but I'm not embarrassed. It's just life, I suppose.

'Here we are!' says Sophie, threading her way back through the tables with a tray piled high with toasted cheese sandwiches, fries and Cokes.

'This place makes the best toasties,' says Jemima, opening up one of hers to put tomato ketchup inside. I smile, thinking how Josh does that too. I am looking forward to seeing him again, and Henry. And even Ed.

'I can't believe you're leaving tomorrow, Juno,' says Sophie, her mouth full of fries. 'It feels like you've been here ages. Mind you, it feels like *I've* been here a hundred years.'

'I know, me too. We'll have to keep in touch,' I add, shyly. 'And maybe – who knows? I might come back next year!'

'Oh, cool,' says Jemima. 'Gap year?'

'Yeah, maybe,' I say, nodding. And smiling. I'm nervous but excited because I really mean it.

We start talking about the application process, and which other ski resorts are meant to be good. We don't talk about Boy. They seem to have forgotten about him, or forgotten that I stayed for him. It's kind of nice. Just like it's nice not to be crowded by questions from Mum.

As I sip my Coke, I start to realise how Boy must have felt – when I was all over *him* with questions and concern. And he was right. He *didn't* ask me to stay; I decided to do it without even asking him. Well, lesson learned. It's just a pity I've learned it too late.

I've drafted a million different texts to him but haven't sent any. Now I wonder if I should say something about how I'm sorry if I crowded him. But then I remember the cruel, cold look in his eyes, and think: no. I didn't deserve that.

'Juno?' Sophie's saying, waving her hand in front of me. 'What do you think for tonight: Buddha Bar or Foxy Fox? Or! We could even try to leave the village?'

'There's a snowstorm forecast for tonight,' says Jemima. 'So I don't think anyone's leaving the village.' She nods towards the horizon where, sure enough, there is a bank of threatening-looking clouds engulfing the blue.

'How about the Foxy Fox for a change?' I suggest. 'Sorry. I just need to send a quick text.'

And before I can over-think it any more, I type out a message to Boy: *It's OK, honestly. Don't worry about it. I hope you get better really soon. Take care. Juno x*

And I guess that's that.

48

Jemima was right about the snowstorm. It starts around five, and by the time we've finished clearing up after dinner – early because it's the last night – it's already several inches deep. We all converge on the Foxy Fox, without even bothering to change out of our uniforms.

'Did you hear?' says Tara. 'Jean-Philippe is out on another date tonight.'

'With who?' asks Sophie.

Tara pauses before delivering her punchline. 'Tabitha! Apparently she's liked him for ages.'

'You're not jealous, are you?' Jemima asks her, with a sly smile.

Tara gives her a look, and we all burst out laughing. I'm glad she's not upset. And I'm glad that Tabitha's going out with Jean-Philippe: I sincerely hope she enjoys her evening of looking at cake pictures.

'I'm off to the bar,' says Lara. 'What does everyone want?'

'Wait, let me give you some money ... Oh no!' I say suddenly. 'I forgot to go to the office to pick up my wages!'

'There should be someone there, if you go now,' says Tara.

'Here, borrow my jacket,' says Lara.

'Thanks,' I say, gratefully muffling myself in her full-length Michelin-man parka, with its hood. If I'm going to do a ski season next year, I'll really have to get proper gear.

After five minutes of walking horizontally into the blizzard, I realise this was really stupid. I'll try to go tomorrow instead, before I leave for the airport. I've just rotated myself back towards the bar – it's hard to see when I turn my head because of my enormous hood – when I notice a familiar silhouette.

It's Boy! But what is he doing here? Why isn't he on crutches? And the desperate hope: has he come here to find me?

I hurry to tap him on the shoulder, but when he turns round my heart sinks. It's not him. This man *looks* very like him, but it's not him. No beard, for a start.

'Yes?' says the person, whoever it is. His voice sounds familiar, too. I know who it is!

'Um, are you Theo? Or Hugh?' I ask.

'Woah,' says the mystery man. 'Spooky. My name *is* Theo. Do I look that much like my ugly brother?'

'Well – no. I mean, yes. I'm a friend of Boy's.'

'Great,' says Theo. 'Maybe you could help me. I'm looking for his place?'

'Oh, he's not here,' I say, dismayed. 'He's at the hospital.'

'Yeah, I know that, don't worry,' Theo smiles. 'I'm picking up some stuff for him. He said it was above a garage, but that doesn't help me much.'

'I can take you there,' I say. 'Except – oh. I need to get to the resort office first, before it closes.'

'Not a problem,' says Theo, indicating a car parked nearby. 'Hop in.'

This is so weird. I'm driving along with Boy's brother to pick up my wages, and then to Boy's garage. I keep sneaking looks at him and marvelling at the similarity, though he's older, and of course, not as cute as Boy.

'Here it is,' I say, pointing. Theo parks and we get out.

'Nice place – not,' Theo mutters, as he takes a key out of his pocket. 'Flipping heck! This is even worse than I imagined.' He switches on the light on his phone, to illuminate the spooky stairwell. 'My little brother lives in the Blair Witch Project.'

'I know,' I say, laughing despite myself, as I put back the hood from my head.

'Hey,' Theo says, looking at me more closely. 'You're Juno, aren't you?'

My eyes widen. 'Yeah! I am. How did you—'

Theo holds up a hand. 'First things first. Let me grab

what I need from this haunted house, before we get snowed in.'

Upstairs, Theo starts opening drawers and efficiently cramming clothes and shoes into a couple of big sports bags. I'm rooted to the spot, memories flooding back. Boy making me tea, talking until late and falling asleep on the sofa together. Watching the sunrise together.

'How is he?' I ask, my voice trembling.

'He's doing well, actually. He got out of bed for the first time today and had a go on crutches. And on Monday he's going to a post-operative facility. Sounds sinister, doesn't it?' Catching sight of my expression, he adds, 'But he'll be fine, don't worry! I'll be with him the whole time. One of the advantages of being an IT geek; you can work from anywhere, mostly.'

'I'm really glad,' I say, sincerely.

Theo pauses, sitting on the arm of Boy's awful sofa. 'Well, *I'm* really glad that you knocked some sense into his head.'

'How d'you mean?'

'There he was, hiding out in hospital without any of us knowing, like the stubborn idiot he is – but then you set him straight. Right?'

'If that's what he said,' I say slowly. So Boy did listen to me after all.

'He did say.' Theo smiles again, looking heart-breakingly like Boy. 'I've never heard Boy talk about anyone the way he talked about you. You've obviously made quite an impression on him.' Looking around, he adds, 'He left something here for you. Wanted me to make sure you got it. Oh, here we go.' And he picks up a plastic bag. A white label on it says 'Joono'.

He must have meant to give it to me on my last night – before his accident. I go to open it, then hesitate.

'Look,' says Theo. 'I gather you've had a fight of some kind, but I think he'd really like to see you. Why don't you come to the hospital tomorrow?'

'I'm leaving tomorrow morning.'

'Oh. Well . . .' Theo frowns, thinking. 'I'm heading back that way now, to my hotel – it's not far from the hospital. I would give you a lift but I'm pretty sure visiting hours are over.'

'No, of course,' I say quickly.

Theo's face changes. 'Actually, who cares about visiting hours? I'm sure we can sneak you in.'

'No, honestly. It's fine. I'll – I'll call him or something.' I clutch the plastic bag to me. 'Thanks for this. And tell him—' Here I'm lost for words. 'Just tell him goodbye.' And I hurry back down the stairs and out into the night.

49

It's coming down so heavily that I'm not even sure I can make it back to the Foxy Fox without becoming a walking snowman; plus, I need a minute to think. I duck into the hostel, and sit down in the hallway to open the parcel from Boy.

Oh. It's my jumper, which I hadn't even missed; I must have left it at his place. I fold it up, trying to swallow my disappointment.

Then I notice something else underneath: a brown paper parcel. I open it up and find a load of small items, wrapped in more brown paper. A compass, matches, a whistle, a pair of plastic walkie-talkies ... and water-purifying tablets.

I start to laugh. It's a Zombie Apocalypse Survival Kit.

And then my laughter turns to a gulp, as I realise I've turned down my last chance to see him again. *Why* didn't I take Theo up on his offer to drive me to the hospital?

I know why. It was the same reason I didn't want to return Boy's phone call: because I was scared. I was scared that Theo was wrong about Boy wanting to see me. I was scared of getting hurt again. And who knows; maybe his feelings *have* changed since he made this present for me.

Still, I've got to take the risk. Which means I have to face my fears.

But I've *already* faced my fears! I faced them on the ski slope the other day. And when I decided to stay here, and so many other times in the past two weeks. And now I have to do it *again*?

That's when it dawns on me. Overcoming my fears isn't one magic moment that changes things for ever. It's something I'll have to do over and over, for the rest of my life. Like going to the dentist.

Well, if that's the case, I'd better make a start.

50

Still clutching my plastic bag, I run back outside, all the way to the garage, but Theo's car is gone. Swallowing my disappointment, I look at the space where it was parked, already filling up with snow. I think I can just about make out his rear lights in the distance.

I hurry forward, waving. 'Theo! Wait!'

But he keeps driving and turns the corner. It's too late; he's gone.

Now what? There won't be any buses, not in this weather. Or taxis. My only hope . . .

My only hope is to borrow a car. And I know who has one.

Tabitha's room is just down the corridor from ours, back at the hostel. To my relief, she's still there and her door is open. She's obviously getting ready for her date: her hair's in a messy top bun and she's doing winged eyeliner. In contrast, I'm red-faced, dripping snow and breathless from all the running around.

'Oh, hi Juno,' she says, seeming unsurprised to see me. 'You look really wet. Is it still snowing outside? So annoying! I had this gorgeous pair of suede boots, but they'll get wrecked. I *could* wear these leather ones, but . . .'

I'm so out of breath I can't even interrupt her. She chatters on about her outfit for what feels like centuries, while I think: I wasn't wrong. She *is* quite superficial. Finally, I manage to get my breath back.

'Tabitha. Could I please borrow your car? I need to get to the hospital. To see Boy,' I add, in case she's going to suggest I call an ambulance. Which would be another option, I suppose.

'Oh,' she says, stopping short, eyeliner in hand.

A strange expression crosses her face – like one of the twins when they think the other one has chosen a better snack or toy. I think I get her now. She's not a bad person – she just keeps her exes close in case she needs a fall-back option.

Luckily, Jean-Philippe seems to have distracted her very effectively.

'Sure,' she says, shrugging. 'Here's the key – it's parked outside.'

'Great. Thank you!' I had thought that there would be all kinds of problems with insurance, or that she'd want to see my licence, but she's obviously not one to worry about those things. I normally would, but not tonight.

'What's the best route?' I could just follow the way the bus goes, but maybe she knows a short-cut.

'Oh. I don't actually know.' She looks guilty. 'I keep meaning to go, but . . .'

'You keep *meaning* to go?'

She says, defensively, 'It's not my fault! Hospitals totally freak me out. I did send him some Kinder eggs.'

I have no words. All my worries about Tabitha and Boy, and she was never even at the hospital. She was too scared. I'll probably look back and laugh about this – someday.

'No worries. Thanks so much,' I add, putting the keys in my pocket. 'I'll give them back tomorrow morning, OK? Have a great time tonight.' And I practically sprint out, before she can change her mind.

Or before I can change *my* mind. I know the route to the hospital in my sleep. And I do have my licence with me, in the spirit of Be Prepared. But I haven't driven much since I passed my test, and I've never driven on the wrong side of the road before – let alone in this kind of weather.

Too late now, though. I'm committed. But first, I duck back into the Foxy Fox, to give Lara her coat back and also let the others know where I'm going.

'The hospital? Now?' says Tara, bemused. 'Why?'

'I have to see him.'

'Fair enough,' she says. 'Do you want us to go with you? For moral support? Or to help you change lanes?'

'Oh, you don't have to . . .' I say hesitantly. 'Well. Are

you sure? Actually, that would be great.' I could do with some back-up.

'Of course we will!' says Lara. 'We'll be your human GPS. I would happily drive but I've already had a glass of wine.'

'Can we come too?' says Sophie. 'I am just dying to—'

'Leave the village!' everyone choruses, while Sophie grins.

'What about us?' asks Mikey, who's just arrived, together with Rob.

'Nope, sorry guys,' says Lara. 'Girls' trip only.'

So we all pile into Tabitha's jeep: Tara in the front with me and Sophie, Jemima and Lara in the back. I've never driven a car this big; it feels as if I'm miles above the ground. Tara has to help me turn the lights and wipers on, and then it takes me ages to reverse. Lara gets out and waves me onwards like a traffic policewoman.

'You can do it, Juno,' Tara says, encouragingly.

'You'll be fine; this baby has snow chains,' says Jemima, patting her arm rest approvingly. 'And everyone will be going slowly, because of the snow.'

We crawl out of the village, and then onto the main road, following the bus route. Jemima was right; everyone is inching along, but the roads are clear and I can see fine. And whenever I feel wobbly, I think of Boy's survival kit in the dashboard, and it gives me a boost.

'Go Juno!' says Sophie as I pull into the hospital car park, and the others all cheer. Thankfully, there are hardly any other cars so my terrible parking doesn't matter.

I did it! I can't believe I drove all this way, on the wrong side of the road, in the snow. Maybe being brave is like driving; it gets easier with practice.

'Thanks, guys,' I say, turning off the engine. 'Listen, I hope you won't be too bored while I'm in here.'

'Are you joking? We're right in the centre of town! We can find a bar, even see a late film . . .' says Sophie. 'How long do you think you'll be?'

This is an excellent question. For all I know, we'll have a five-minute conversation and that will be that. Or I won't be allowed in at all; it's almost ten o'clock. Or maybe Theo was wrong and he won't want to see me at all.

Biting my lip, I admit, 'I have absolutely no idea.'

51

The hospital's almost deserted, and it is well after visiting hours. Luckily, Karin, the nurse I've met before, is on duty and she lets me slip by. As I approach Boy's room, though, I feel more nervous than I ever have before in my life. What if he's asleep? I'm not going to wake him up.

But he's awake. He's listening to my MP3 player. When I knock on the door, he looks up and stares at me. I'm a total mess; I'm dripping melting snow all over the floor, and my hair is clinging to my face in tendrils – but from the slow, incredulous smile that spreads over his face, I could be wearing a ball gown.

'Juno.' It's all he needs to say.

I don't even think twice. I hurry forward into his arms. He holds me tight, and I hold him tighter.

'I'm really sorry,' he says, in between kissing my hair. 'I was such a git.'

'No – well, yes, you were. But maybe I should have given you more space.' I disentangle myself to look at him.

'No. No way,' he says, shaking his head. 'The thing is . . . Can I explain?'

'Of course.'

He sighs. 'I know it sounds lame but . . . this accident has been my worst nightmare. Not just the pain or losing my job, but having to depend on other people. I've basically set my whole life up so that I don't have to depend on anyone. Especially not my dad. And now I'm completely helpless. And it's terrifying.'

I nod slowly.

'So the reason I was so horrible to you . . . it wasn't because I didn't think I needed help. It was because I knew I did, and I hated it. *Hated* it.' He swallows. 'So I took it out on you, and I'm sorry.'

'But what about Tabitha?'

He frowns. 'What about her?'

'It just hurt that you were able to talk to her but not to me.'

His face clears. 'But I didn't! Not really. I told her in a text that I hadn't called my family. But that was because I knew she didn't care that much. And I didn't really care what she thought, either.'

'Oh.'

'She was never going to make me face up to the situation the way you did.' He looks at me seriously. 'It's true that I didn't ask you to stay. But I'm lucky you did.'

225

His hand comes out to grab mine, and I grab his, tightly. He pulls me up and we kiss for the longest time. When we stop, I can see that his eyes are suspiciously red.

'Do you know what else?' he says, clearing his throat. 'It really helped me, what you said. About how we have to band together because of the zombies.'

'What? Oh! Why?'

'Because it made me feel better about needing other people. It made me feel like it's less about me being pathetic . . . and more of a survival strategy. So I called my brother Theo.'

'Yes! I met him earlier, in the village.' I won't even get into my whole journey here. 'So what's going to happen after you leave hospital?'

'I'll be moving back to Bristol, with Theo. He's going to put me up in his daughter's playroom during my rehab. All the Lego I could want. Plus, he's handling my dad for me, giving him information on a need-to-know basis. It actually hasn't been so bad.'

He looks so happy that I can't help asking, 'Why didn't you talk to Theo before?'

'I didn't want to be a pain. Or maybe I was too scared?' He smiles. 'Not everyone's as brave as you, you know.'

'As brave as me?'

'Sure.' His brown eyes are serious. 'When the apocalypse comes . . . I want you on my team.'

I'm bubbling over with so much joy, I could touch the ceiling.

'I got your survival kit, by the way,' I say.

'Good. Did you see the plastic walkie-talkie? It might help us keep in touch.'

'Yes. Or we could phone, or Skype.'

'Sure.' He pauses, and adds questioningly, 'There are also frequent buses from Bristol to London. I'm sure they would survive a zombie attack. If we wanted to try them?'

I stop to catch my breath. Are we actually doing this? It looks like we are.

'Sure. Let's meet up in one of those places – once my A levels are over.'

'Or once the apocalypse hits. Whichever is first.'

He draws me closer, until our foreheads are touching, and then he tilts my mouth up to meet his.

A while later he says, 'Look. It's stopped snowing.'

Glancing out of the window, I see that he's right. I sigh contentedly and settle back down on his shoulder. I feel as if we've been inside one of those toy globes, whirled upside down in a snowstorm, and now the snow has finally settled to reveal the two of us exactly where we're meant to be.

Epilogue

'Juno!' Mum calls up the stairs. 'Boy called.'

'Oh! Did he?' I run back down, taking one earphone out and rubbing my eyes. I've spent the afternoon in the park with Emma and Ruby, and I've got that sun-dazed sleepy haze going on, plus at least twenty extra freckles because I forgot my sunscreen. 'What did he say?'

'Just the usual,' Mum says. 'To say that he called. I don't mind taking messages, but just out of interest – does he never ring your mobile?'

'I like that he calls the landline,' Ed says, appearing beside her. 'It's like we did in the olden days.' He squeezes Mum's shoulders and I pretend to roll my eyes at them both.

'Exactly,' I tell Ed. 'He's old-fashioned.' The truth is that Boy gets free calls to landlines with his new phone. But we also Skype, and he's even joined WhatsApp.

'Will you be ready soon, Ju?' Mum asks. 'The table's booked for eight.'

It's over two weeks since my A levels ended, but this is our official celebration – with Mum and Ed, that is. I celebrated last week with Dad, and the week before – obviously – with Emma, Ruby and Mia.

'Juno!' Henry's just zoomed into the room, sliding in his socks. 'Are you going to Skype Boy soon? I have a new magic trick to show him.'

'Oh, great! He will love that.'

'Are you going to put your shoes on any time soon, Henrico?' Ed asks him. 'It's nearly pizza time.'

'PizZA! PizZA!' says Josh, running past us at top speed.

'I'll be down soon,' I promise. 'I just want to email Tara.'

Running up to my room, I shut the door and curl up on my bed with my laptop. I've grown to love my room. I've added more and more of my own things – a postcard of Cork, a film poster of *Gone With the Wind*, a photo of Boy and a picture of Dad. I know it won't be home for ever, but for now it's a good place to be.

Hi Tara,
How are you? Thailand looks amazing! All of your pictures are like screensavers. I'm fine, very happy to have finished exams. I think they went OK, but at this stage, I don't even care. They're over. And I start work next week in a French restaurant on

Upper Street so I'll be putting all my chalet skills to
good work!

Thanks for asking about Boy. He's working like
mad at his rehab – physio three times a week,
swimming, no more smoking, even acupuncture
if you can imagine Boy doing that. It's been very
tough and he's had lots of low moments. But he and
his dad are getting on better – they've even started
going fishing together, and Boy says he's no longer
tempted to push him underwater.

I pause and smile as I think of all the other things
that have happened with Boy. He's also working on his
reading and writing. And I've even found out his real
name. It's Arthur. Like so many things, it's not what I'd
imagined but I really like it.

I've decided to change my course to law. Instead
of worrying about the environment and doing
nothing, I'm going to be an environmental lawyer.
And I'm definitely taking a year out, hopefully
starting with a ski season. After that, I'm not
sure. Boy and I have talked about doing a big trip
together next summer before I start uni. It's a long
way away but who knows? Stranger things have
happened . . .

Write back soon. Say hi to the dolphins for me!
Lots of love
Juno x

Re-reading my email to Tara, I feel a little embarrassed as I notice how much of it is about Boy. I'm about to erase those parts, but then I change my mind and press send. She'll understand. Also, I'll be writing to her again – and I have a feeling life is about to get a lot more exciting.

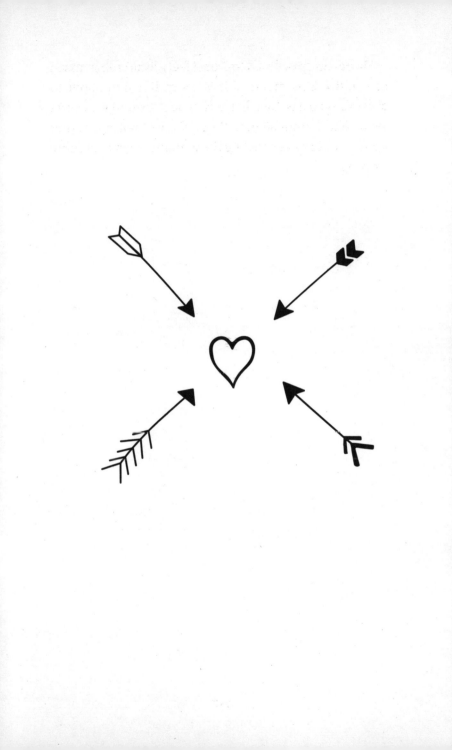

Acknowledgements

I was lucky to work with two fantastic editors on this book – Jenny Glencross, who first suggested I should write for teens, and Felicity Johnston, who pushed me, with great tact and enthusiasm, to make this a far better story than I realised it could be. Thanks also to Thy Bui and Sinem Erkas for the beautiful cover art, and to the whole team at Indigo.

I am indebted to Laura Holleman, who shared her experience of spiral fractures with me. Thanks also to Hermione Ruck-Keene for putting us in touch. Thank you to Sile Edwards, who gave me a very valuable perspective on the story and also explained the difference between a gif and a vine. My brother Gavan provided ski trivia, and Anne Vial helped with German phrases. Boy's Everest anecdote was inspired by Fergus White's *Ascent into Hell*, which I'd recommend to anyone who wants to know what that climb is really like (horrendous, in a word). Any factual mistakes are my own.

As ever none of this would have happened without my superhero agent, Rowan Lawton – a massive thank you to her and to her daring sidekick Liane-Louise Smith.

I hate to think what would happen to me or my books without Alex. Thank you for listening to my cries of 'I can't do this' and 'It will never be finished.' When the Apocalypse comes, I want you on my team.

This book is dedicated to my mother, who when I was fourteen and traumatised by the news, told me to remember all the planes that *don't* crash and the people who *don't* get murdered. Great advice, as always – thank you, Mum.

Nicola Doherty
North London
January 2016

Nicola also writes romantic comedies for adults.
Visit www.nicoladohertybooks.com to find out more.

And read on for a sneak preview of her next YA novel,

Girl Offline . . .

1

If you ever find yourself internationally notorious, and about to go on the run, I highly recommend not having a name like Delilah Hoover.

I've never liked my name, obviously. The whole sucking thing; enough said. But the worst thing is its findability. Before the story broke, there were about 350,000 search results for Delilah Hoover, and most of them related to vacuum cleaners. (Disclaimer: other brands are available). Now there are over three million. And they're all about me.

For a few weeks, I was famous. I was trending on Twitter. There were blog posts about me, newspaper articles even. But the worst things of all were the comments. I only saw a couple before Mum and Dad took my phone and laptop away, but that was more than enough. I was internationally notorious. And it really sucked.

2

'Are you sure you want to do this, love?' said Mum.

I looked up from trying to squash my furry monster-paw slippers into my suitcase. 'What – go to Paris? Of course I'm sure! And we agreed it!' Fear bubbled in my stomach. 'You haven't changed your mind, have you?'

We'd already discussed this, months ago, at a two-hour 'family summit' over pizza. Motion for discussion: Should Delilah be allowed transfer to an international school in Paris? Mum and Dad were against the motion. My little brother Lenny was for it, but that was because he was heartless and also loved change – any change. In the end they said it was my decision. Which is what people say when they think you're making a terrible mistake.

'I know we agreed it,' said Mum. 'But it seems so drastic. I'm sure everything here will blow over . . .'

I said nothing, because we both knew that wasn't

true. The university had withdrawn their offer of a place. I was still afraid to go back online. No blowing-over from where I sat; not even a little breeze.

'But what about your friends? I'm sure they'll miss you . . .'

I was even less sure about that. Things had been weird with them since it happened, even Ellie. She *said* she didn't care about it – they all did: her, Jules and Nisha. But they'd also been to Glastonbury without telling me. Where, according to Instagram, they all got matching daisy face paint and Jules had met a boy. Big deal.

'I'm positive,' I said, kneeling on my suitcase to try and make it close. For someone with no clothes, I'd found it very hard to pack. Of course I *had* clothes, I just didn't like any of them. They all felt like the discarded snake-skins of my past selves, as I'd written pretentiously in my diary the night before. There were the hideous mistakes, like my long black skirt and white lace blouse from when I wanted to look like a Victorian governess; or the Great Catsby sweater I tracked down online after seeing Taylor Swift wear it. I wasn't sure if any of my clothes were really me. But then I didn't want to be me any more, so maybe that was a good thing.

'Stop – let me help you.' Mum leaned forward easily from her cross-legged position, and held the case down while I zipped it. She'd always been into yoga, but she started doing it even more when everything kicked off – and reading inspirational books, and even meditating. If she became a Buddhist monk, it would all be my fault.

'Think how good it will be for my French,' I said, to cheer her up. 'And I might pick up other languages. I might become fluent in Tagalog!'

'Tagalog? That's not a real language, is it?'

'Yes! It's what they speak in the Philippines.'

'OK, OK.'

Languages were my thing: I collected phrases from other languages the way other people collected selfie likes. So far I could speak French, Spanish and Mandarin (though my Mandarin was shaky) plus smatterings of lots more. I'd even made up my own language, Delilish. So far, Lenny and I were the only native speakers, though Ellie had picked up some basics.

'It's just the boarding thing, really, that seems sad to me,' Mum said, with a sigh.

'It'll be fine,' I said breezily, to hide the fact that I was terrified. 'Look, Mum, I'll be back for Easter. It's not that long.'

'Don't worry! Take as long as you need.' It was Lenny, barrelling in without knocking as usual. Taking out a tape measure, he started measuring my bedroom walls.

'What do you think you're doing?' I said.

'I'm checking my stuff will fit in here. Mum said I could, didn't you Mum?'

'I said *maybe. If* your sister agrees. His room is really small,' Mum said, looking harassed. 'And when he's got all his gaming friends over –'

'Don't worry, I won't change too much,' Lenny said. 'I

really like what you've done with it. Just think it needs more of a man's touch.'

My impulse was to pick him up by the scruff of his hoody and ping him out of my room, but I was trying to be less impulsive. Since that was what got me into trouble in the first place.

'Fine,' I said. 'Have it. Just clear out when I come home, and *don't* use my sheets.'

Lenny's mouth dropped into a startled O. With a pang, I realised he hadn't just wanted to get under my skin; he'd wanted me to react to him. Maybe it was his weird way of showing he would miss me.

'Seriously, Len,' I said. 'Be my *guest*.' I gave him a hug, normally a guaranteed way of getting rid of him. Instead he started doing parkour around my room, until Mum shooed him out. That was typical Lenny; he recovered quickly. At least I didn't have to worry about him.

'Hey!' Dad said, appearing in the doorway. 'So . . . you're doing your packing.'

'Yep.' I nodded, mirroring his awkward smile.

'Great.'

Most of my chats with Dad in the past few months had followed this pattern. 'So . . . you're having your breakfast.'

'Yep.'

'Great.'

Awkward smiles. Silence.

To try and spice things up, I added, 'I don't think it will be that cold in Paris, but I'm not sure.'

He took out his phone, relieved to have a distraction. 'Siri! Check weather in Paris.'

Dad was so devoted to Siri, I was surprised he hadn't included her in our family conference. He obviously found her much easier to talk to than me.

'I'm sorry, I didn't get that,' said Siri.

'Siri!' Dad barked. 'Check! Weather! In Paris!'

'OK. Checking for you now,' said Siri.

'Shouldn't you say please?' said Mum.

'Why on earth would I say please? It's a robot.'

'Shh!' said Mum. 'She'll hear you.'

I cleared my throat. 'Mum. Dad. I've decided something else.'

They both turned to me, with the identical worried expressions that had become so familiar.

'I'm changing my name. To Lola.'

'But why–' Mum said, before closing her mouth. She knew why.

'Are you sure the school will let you change your name?' Dad said.

'You saw the form they sent – child's name, child prefers to be known as. Lola is sort of a nickname for Delilah. And I can use your surname,' I added, to Mum.

'Lola Maxwell – not bad,' said Dad.

'Lola is awful! It sounds like a stripper,' said Mum. *Unlike Delilah?* I thought. 'Surely we can think of something better.' Now she and Dad both had their phones out.

'Siri! Suggestions for girls' names!'

'OK. Checking for you now.'

Dad looked up. 'What about your middle name?' he said hopefully.

'Dad!'

'Steve!'

Mum and I spoke in unison. My middle name is Uhura. What can I say? Dad is a Star Trek fan. Not the Next Generation, and definitely not the films, just the original series which . . . Never mind. It's too boring.

'Look, darling, if you want you can call yourself Lola,' Mum said quickly. 'Just for this year. But you can't change it forever, you know.'

I wanted to tell her it *was* forever – but something stopped me. Maybe it was the sight of the new lines around Mum's eyes despite all the organic skin cream she bought, or the fact that Dad's fingers were always drumming nervously these days, when he wasn't talking to Siri.

They didn't have the option of moving to Paris, or changing their names. My parents weren't international people of mystery; they were a worried-looking biology teacher and IT consultant. A lump was growing in my throat as I thought how much I was going to miss them. And how ashamed I was that I had done this to them.

I looked around my room, crammed with the junk of years: all my books, from *The Baby-Sitters Club* to Jane Austen, my ancient Keep Calm poster, my bean bag collapsing in front of my laptop and Flossie, my pink flamingo light. Not to mention old nail varnishes, discarded necklaces and neon eyeshadows from my experimental make-up phase. It was going to take a while to clear it all out for Lenny, but I would do it. I'd erase every trace of myself and their lives would be a whole lot easier.

3

By now, I'm sure you're wondering what it was, exactly, that I did. Don't worry. This isn't going to be one of those times where you wait until you're 90% through and then find out I stole a traffic cone or something. I will tell you, and soon. But here's what I didn't do.

1. It was nothing sexual (I wish. The closest I've come to sending a sexy picture was when I had to email the dermatologist a picture of my mole.)
2. I didn't kill a lion.
3. Or put a cat in a bin.
4. I didn't hurt anyone. At least not physically.
5. I didn't break any laws.
6. I just made a stupid mistake.

And now I was paying for it. Every day I regretted it; I feel horrible and worthless and a pathetic excuse of a person. I wished I was anybody but me. But maybe that wish was about to come true.